TRAIL TO ELSEWHERE

After seven-year-old Brad and his younger sister Julie are orphaned, they are separated and adopted by different families miles apart. As they grow up, each must face their own challenges: Brad's new brother Saul is hostile and brutal, while Julie, treated as a drudge, sees her only means of escape in marrying a man she does not love. Then Saul falls into criminality with the Coyote Gang. An altercation between the brothers lands Brad in jail — and Saul's path is about to cross with Julie's . . .

*Books by Walter L. Bryant
in the Linford Western Library:*

NINE DEAD MEN
THE PREACHER'S LEGACY

WALTER L. BRYANT

TRAIL TO ELSEWHERE

Complete and Unabridged

LINFORD
Leicester

First published in Great Britain in 2014 by
Robert Hale Limited
London

First Linford Edition
published 2016
by arrangement with
Robert Hale Limited
London

A catalogue record for this book is available
from the British Library.

ISBN 978–1–4448–2823–8

Published by
F. A. Thorpe (Publishing)
Anstey, Leicestershire

Set by Words & Graphics Ltd.
Anstey, Leicestershire
Printed and bound in Great Britain by
T. J. International Ltd., Padstow, Cornwall

This book is printed on acid-free paper

Prologue

'What's yer name, son?'

At the sound of the strange voice Brad looked up to find himself being scrutinized by a man roughly dressed in dungarees, blue shirt and working boots. Whiskers covered the lower half of his face. The man laid a hand on his shoulder.

The voice had not been unfriendly, and Brad felt a little lifting of his spirits as kindly eyes looked into his. He had been told to answer firmly and promptly.

'Brad, sir.'

'How old are you?'

'Nearly eight, sir.'

Brad Harris had had the misfortune of being born in New York in 1861 to parents who had few means and no intention of keeping him.

By the age of seven he and his

younger sister, Julie, were orphans, homeless and without hope on the city streets. Brad took care of his sister, never letting her out of his sight. For her part Julie clung on as they begged and stole in order to survive.

For over six months they had scratched a living in this way. Then, in a matter of moments, their fortunes changed. They were taken to a large building where they were bathed and fed and given a place to sleep.

Eventually, they were uprooted once more from the surroundings they knew, put on a train and transported along with many other children through unfamiliar country towards the American Midwest.

The journey was long and tiring. At first the anticipation of a new adventure kept Brad's spirits up, but gradually reality set in as the distance from the mean streets of the city increased. He became scared, thirsty and hungry.

Time passed in a dream, until eventually the children were ushered from the confines of the stuffy carriages to stand on a platform at the edge of the small township of Elsewhere. They were bewildered by the noise and inquisitive gaze of men and women who had clearly been waiting for them. The huge train belched black smoke from its front end, and then seemed to settle down like a sleeping monster.

Unaccustomed smells filled Brad's nostrils, strange noises assailed his ears. He tried to shut them all out so that he could think clearly.

Brad's sister, one year younger, stood beside him, shivering in spite of the overwhelming heat. They held hands, reaping strength from the presence of each other. They had remained together, inseparable, for the duration of the journey.

'You look as if ya could do with a bath an' a hot meal,' a man said, running his hands over Brad's arms. 'Need buildin' up, too, I reckon.'

Brad nodded, not sure whether he was supposed to respond.

The man turned to another, taller gentleman who was well dressed, wearing a large, drooping moustache and was busy writing something in a book. 'He'll do.'

He took hold of Brad's arm and tried to ease him away from his sister. Brad tightened his grip on Julie's hand and held on.

'Sorry, son,' the man said. 'We kin only take you. Another home'll be found fer yer sister. It'll be OK.'

But Brad didn't reckon it would be OK. 'We stay together,' he said, his voice rising as he struggled to make himself heard above the noise.

'Can't be done. One's all we kin manage.'

Brad felt their hands being disengaged, and struggled as Julie was guided away from him.

'No,' he screamed, and kicked out.

Julie screwed her head round towards her brother, her eyes wet with tears, her mouth opening, unable to form words. Brad looked pleadingly at the other people but, although some smiled reassuringly at him, none came to his aid. When he turned again he saw that his sister was being taken back on to the train. He continued to struggle, but to no avail.

'Don't worry, Brad. She'll be OK,' the man said again. 'We're gonna take you home now. You're gonna have a new place to live.'

The man's hand was large and rough on his own young skin. Brad's other hand was held in a softer grip, and for the first time he noticed that a woman had joined the man, and that he was being conducted away. Although he was still fighting, fear and despair were weakening his efforts to resist.

Everything now seemed to be happening inside his head rather than around him: the hiss of steam, the voices, the rattle of wagon wheels, the clatter of hoofs, the heavy smells of smoke, horses and people. The woman spoke softly into his ear, but he wasn't listening.

He allowed himself to be helped up on to the front seat of a wagon, from where he twisted round for a last despairing look at the train where he was sure Julie was being held prisoner.

'Where're we going?' he asked, fearful now of the unknown.

'Home,' the woman replied with a reassuring smile. 'You're going home.'

The two horses hauled the wagon away from the bustle of the station and, in spite of himself, Brad was fascinated by the rhythm and movement of the hindquarters of the animals. There had been horses in New York for sure, but none as sleek and powerful as these.

They soon left the buildings behind and travelled through open country. Brad had seen this kind of terrain through the carriage windows, but now that he was part of it the horizon seemed to stretch away for ever. He remained quiet as the wagon rattled on, ignoring any attempts to involve him in conversation.

Nevertheless he listened, and learned

that the man's name was Sam Finnan and that the woman was his wife, Sadie. He was told that he was being taken to a farm, and that he would be treated as one of the family. He wasn't reassured; all his thoughts were on Julie. How would she cope without him?

'I wanna be with my sister,' he said at last.

Sam Finnan looked at his wife, then back at Brad. 'Yer sister's prob'ly hunnerds o' miles away by now,' he said gently.

From his journey in the train Brad had gleaned some idea of the vastness of this land, but he only had a vague notion of what hundreds of miles looked like. He knew only that it was a great distance.

'I want my sister,' he repeated, this time with tears welling up in his eyes.

Sadie laid a hand on Brad's shoulder. 'We know you do,' she said. 'It's not possible. It must've bin explained to you. She'll find another family. Best if you try to put her outa your mind.'

'I won't!' Brad bit his lip until it bled. 'We've always bin together.' His voice was hoarse with anger and frustration. 'You'll see. I'll find her.'

'You'll forget in time, you'll see. Maybe we should give you a new name now you've got a new family.'

'My name's Brad!'

'Right, Brad it shall be.'

After several hours of travelling Brad saw ahead of them a low, white-painted house set in the shelter of a stand of trees. A rill ran along the back beyond the outhouses and there was a fenced-off area containing horses.

Sam pointed. 'We're there,' he said. 'This is where you're gonna live. This is yer new home. You'll be happy here, able to go to school and learn.'

Brad had no intention of staying long enough to be happy or to learn, but when he looked around he wondered if he would ever be able to leave. Where would he go? He was used to streets full of movement, buildings side by side in long rows. And noise. Here there was the silence of eternity except for the unfamiliar sounds of cattle in the distance, and other noises he couldn't immediately identify.

As they approached, a boy came out of the house. He was, Brad guessed, about nine or ten, tall and well-built, tanned from an outdoor life. He scowled up at his parents.

'Our son, Saul,' Sam said.

Brad relaxed a little. It looked as if he wouldn't be alone here.

As they alighted from the wagon Saul took charge of the horses and led them away.

'Saul,' Sam called. 'Take Brad with you. Show him round the place. You two might as well get to know each other.'

Saul didn't pause. Brad ran to catch up with the other boy, and then walked beside him.

'A mite thin, ain't ya,' Saul sneered. 'If yer reckon to stay here ya'll have to take yer share of the hard work.'

'I'm not staying,' Brad said, confused

by the reception he was getting.

'That's good, then.' Saul grinned. 'I sure don't want ya.'

'I'm gonna find my sister.'

Saul's mouth split into a wicked grin. 'If ya need a nursemaid I'll sure as hell be happy to take on that role. I've always reckoned to have a slave o' my own.'

'I don't need lookin' after an' I don't want nothin' to do with you.' Brad stopped, turned and began to walk back towards the house.

'Stay where you are,' Saul roared. 'You go when I tell ya. You do as I tell ya. From now on you do nothin' 'less I say so. Yer not gonna worm yer way into this family. You're a farmhand like the others here. Unnerstood?' He let go of the horses.

Brad kept on walking until he felt a strong grip on his shoulder which spun him round. He looked up into Saul's face and saw anger there. He twisted free.

Saul grabbed at him again and this

time it hurt as fingers dug into his flesh.

'Let me go!' Brad lashed out, and by luck his knuckles glanced off Saul's nose. There was little damage done, but it was enough to make Saul bunch his fist and drive it into Brad's chest.

'You wanna fight me?' he snarled. He took on the stance of a boxer, feet dancing, fists moving threateningly.

Saul was big for his age and powerful, but years on the city streets had taught Brad how to fight. And it was not in the way that Saul clearly expected. He darted in and landed a kick in Saul's groin that made the older boy double up in pain.

'I don't want to fight you,' Brad said, stepping back out of reach of Saul's flailing arms. He picked up a large stone and held it threateningly, as he waited for Saul to recover.

'Goddamn it!' Saul screamed. In three strides he had reached the younger boy, ducking to avoid the stone that was aimed at his head. In spite of that the stone hit him on the ear. He hardly paused as his momentum took him and Brad to the ground.

At close quarters they wrestled, and for a while Brad gave as good as he received, feeling some satisfaction when his teeth sank into Saul's hand. Although he managed a few punishing strikes with head and fists, he was overwhelmed by the superior strength of the older boy. His face was pushed into the dirt, vicious blows rained on to his arms and body. He tasted blood and spat dirt from his mouth.

'Had enough?' Saul grated. 'Now you know who's boss around here.'

Brad felt a hand take hold of his hair. His head was pulled up and slammed back into the ground. Several times this was repeated until he felt his senses reeling. For the space of a minute the world went black. Then he was roughly hauled up, slung over Saul's shoulder and carried like a sack of corn towards the house.

'Listen to me, you little piece of crow bait,' Saul was saying. 'I know yer listenin'. If ya tell Ma an' Pa what happened out here you'll get more o' the same, only worse. From now on I'll make ya my slave.'

Brad remained silent. He heard Sadie gasp when she saw them. 'What happened? You both look like you've been in a fight.'

'Sorry, Ma,' Saul said. 'He jumped into the corral afore I could stop him. That chestnut mare's still wild, an' I had to go in an' pull him out.'

'Thank the Good Lord you did,' Sadie said, although she sounded doubtful at his explanation. 'Lay him down here and I'll see to his injuries before your pa gets back. He'll be none too pleased.'

Brad allowed her to sponge his wounds, and tried not to flinch when she touched his sore arms. He opened his eyes and looked up into Sadie's face. There he fancied he saw a kindness he had not known for a long time. He thought that, perhaps in spite of the older boy, he might like it here.

13

'I'm sorry, Brad,' Sadie said, 'that this should happen on your first day. Perhaps you've learned a lesson about horses.'

He tried to smile but his lips were swollen.

'Listen to what Saul tells you in future and you won't go far wrong.'

He did manage a lopsided smile this time.

His reluctance to tell the truth was not as a result of Saul's threat. He was used to taking care of himself, fighting his own battles and protecting his sister when the need arose.

He would deal with this situation in his own way in his own time.

As he stood he noticed for the first time a young girl, no more than six years old, staring at him.

'You're very skinny,' she said.

Her ma waggled a reproving finger at her. 'Now, Kate, that's not a polite thing to say to your new brother. We'll soon fatten him up.'

'Don't matter,' Brad said. 'I been

14

called all sorts of names before now.'

Kate grinned cheekily at him, showing where one of her front teeth was missing, and Brad felt his heart sink as he was reminded of Julie, who would now be far away. Would he ever see her again?

1

In the twelve years since Julie had been set down at Redstone Creek and taken to her new home, the town had expanded and now held one bank, two saloons, a marshal's office, several eating places and a cluster of stores.

It also had one lawyer. His name was Crichton Randolph who, at thirty-two years of age, still retained his youthful good looks. He was all of six feet in height, clean-shaven with thick, black hair slicked back, and was immaculately dressed in suit, white shirt and cravat. He was sought after by many of the young ladies, who saw him as the ideal husband: wealthy, influential and with great prospects.

He was sitting in his office, staring angrily at the man seated in the chair at the other side of his desk.

'You shouldn't've come here,' he

grated. 'I've told you before it's not good for people to know we're associated.'

His visitor was an older man whose round face, short stature and serious expression gave him the appearance of a trusted bank manager, minister or senator. He was certainly none of those. He was an expert in his chosen profession: confidence trickster, con artist, bunko man, who could sell venom to a rattlesnake. His name was Charles Hinckley.

He was relaxed now as he helped himself to a cigar, struck a vesta and held the flame to the tip. When it was going well he blew out a mouthful of smoke and spoke quietly.

'Give me what's mine an' you won't be troubled by me again.'

Crichton rubbed his chin thoughtfully. 'We've worked well together for how long?'

'Two years by my reckoning.'

'Why stop now?'

'Men who do the kind of work I do

can't stay in one place for long. You know that. We've made ourselves rich, but there're those who're becoming a mite suspicious an' I can't risk the law looking into my life.'

'How do the others feel about this?' Crichton asked.

'I ain't told them yet but I hear rumblings. They kin make up their own minds. All I want is my share o' the takin's. Quite considerable by my reckoning.'

Crichton took a ledger from the safe, carefully closing the heavy metal door before returning to his desk and thumbing through the pages. 'Yeah, I figure you've got over five thousand dollars comin' to you.'

Charles blinked hard. 'Sounds good to me.'

Crichton smiled. He could have told the man any figure. It wouldn't have mattered, because he wasn't going to live long enough to enjoy it. 'That's agreed, then? You keep this to yerself.'

Charles nodded vigorously. 'Ya have my word on it.'

Crichton nodded as if he was satisfied. 'OK. If you've made up your mind about this.'

'I have. Just remember, if the law catches up with me I won't be the only one facin' jail or a lynching.'

Crichton's mind churned. 'I said OK, didn't I? I'll give you your share, but we'll have to meet up later after I get access to the money.'

'How much later?'

'Tomorrow night. Just after sundown outside the livery. It's dark there. We mustn't be seen together after this.' And, he thought, Old Joe's as deaf as a post. He stood, signifying that the meeting was at an end. 'Go out the back door. Make sure nobody sees you.'

After his visitor had left he sat back in his leather chair and considered the options he now had. Was it time for him to quit? There had to be at least $100,000 in the second safe that he had hidden beneath the floorboards in his office. Maybe as much as double that. He hadn't counted it lately. It wasn't all his, of course. Some of it rightly belonged to Charles Hinckley and the other two conmen in his team. But they were not going to see any of it, either.

He had already outlaid some of the money, to keep his investors hooked and to encourage other potential clients. But he knew that, as the stream of new investors dried up, it was time to quit and to vanish with the profits. Perhaps such a time had now come and Crichton acknowledged the fact with a shrug of his shoulders.

Of course, he had other irons in the fire. There was the highly profitable Land Sale scheme that he had built on the rumour of a new railroad spur, and the fake share certificates from the New International Hardrock Consolidated Mining Company.

Both of these had brought him wealth; still did, and might continue to do so. But for how long? Had they run their course? No sense in being too greedy. To take the money and disappear before his customers demanded their money back seemed to be the most sensible course of action.

After an hour of contemplation he had reached a decision. The total amount, $100,000 or more, was not enough to share, just sufficient to support himself and his young wife for a good while.

He replaced the ledger, and with a wry smile contemplated his next moves. There was much to be done if he was to prepare himself for a long journey. He reached into the desk drawer, withdrew a double-barrelled Derringer, checked it over carefully and loaded it. One shot should be enough to dispatch Charles Hinckley to the hereafter, but you couldn't be too careful.

He slipped the weapon into his pocket, checking that there was no telltale bulge.

He next gave thought to his plans for an early marriage. The problem was that the girl of his choice had not yet agreed to become his wife. He sat for a long time considering what he could do to hasten the decision. At length he arose with a wide grin lighting up his face, and left the office in search of two young men who went by the names of Cas and Rufus.

★   ★   ★

Julie had been less fortunate than Brad with her new family. After she had been put back in the carriage she sat in a corner and neither spoke nor moved. She shuddered and moaned quietly to herself as she felt the train pull away from the station.

She had no idea of the passage of time or light and dark. She ate when she was told to, drank when she was thirsty, and slept fitfully when she had to. She had no idea whether she had travelled ten miles or 1,000, leaving Brad behind for ever.

Everything that followed went by in a blur, without meaning, as if in a nightmare. This continued after the train had pulled into Redstone Creek and she was taken on to the platform and led away.

'I want my brother,' Julie said. When that received no response she repeated over and over, 'I want my brother. I want to go home.'

'That's where we're takin' ya,' her new pa said. 'Home. Ya startin' a new life with us. You've gotta forget where ya came from. Forget ya brother. Be grateful we agreed to take ya. Nobody else seemed to want ya.'

Julie curled up and sobbed. She was alone for the first time in her life.

During the years that followed, no love developed between Julie and her new parents. She survived the hard work that was expected of her and the occasional beatings in the early days, and settled into an acceptable life, attending school two or three days a week.

She enjoyed in particular the times, like now, that she could have to herself, driving the buckboard into the town, a ten-mile ride, to get supplies and deliver the farm produce. She loved the scents of the open grassland, the colours of the distant mountains, the rhythmical sounds made by the horse's hoofs and the comforting rattle of the wheels over hard ground.

The day was warm, but the light breeze played on her skin and teased her hair.

'Where ya goin'?' The harsh voice broke into her reverie while she was still a mile from the outskirts of the town.

Two young men on horseback had drawn in beside her and had adjusted their pace to hers. She knew who they were and her heart sank. Rufus and Cas, wild boys who had imposed themselves upon her on several occasions. With her good humour and warm smile she could deal with most men whose heads were turned by her beauty, but these two were different. And now they had intruded on her peace and spoiled her time of tranquillity.

'What's that to you?' She kept her voice level. To show fear to these men merely encouraged them.

'These are perilous times,' Rufus said, showing his teeth. 'There are bad men hereabouts. A young woman travellin' on her own needs protection.'

Cas moved his horse closer and leered into her face. He reached over and took the reins from her hands, then climbed on to the seat next to her. 'So we're offerin' our services.'

She moved away from him. 'I can handle it by myself,' she said and was annoyed that her voice shook a little.

'Yeah, I reckon as how ya can, but I haven't bin so close to a pretty woman fer, well, since the last time.' He roared with laughter and placed a hand on her leg.

She slapped it away. 'Go find someone who enjoys the company of rattlesnakes,' she grated. 'And leave me alone.' She wrested the reins back.

'Oh, we cain't do that. We're gentlemen, ya see, an' we'll see ya get to town without any trouble.'

Julie kept the smile of derision from her face, gazed straight ahead and set the bay to a faster gait. Rufus adjusted the pace of his own horse to keep up.

This time Julie reckoned that, either through drink or bravado, these two were not going to be deterred.

The outskirts of the town appeared ahead and she kept the bay moving. 'Thank you,' she said, politely. 'You can see I'm quite safe now.'

Cas remained on the seat of the buckboard. 'Reckoned yer might've wanted to show yer appreciation in a different way.'

She took a deep breath. 'I want you to go. I'm sure you wouldn't want me to tell Marshal McQuade that you've been harassing me.'

Rufus guffawed. 'The marshal's no trouble.'

'I reckon she'll wanna thank us fer takin' such care of her,' Cas smirked. He took the reins from her and pulled the bay into the cover of some trees.

Rufus grinned. 'Yeah, she'll wanna do that all right. This place'll do jus' fine.'

Cas grabbed Julie's arm and pulled her so that they both toppled backwards over the rear of the seat and ended up on the floor of the buckboard. Rufus joined them.

'Leave me alone!' she screamed, struggling to free herself.

There was nobody to come to her aid. She knew she would not be able to fight off two strong young men intent on doing her harm. But she wasn't about to give in without a struggle. She had not forgotten completely how to fight. With nails, teeth, knees and elbows she inflicted some damage, but the outcome was inevitable.

She was held down by overpowering strength and she gritted her teeth at what she knew was about to happen.

2

'Stop!' A voice, loud and authoritative, caused Cas and Rufus to swivel round to find the source of the command, while they retained their hold on their prey.

A man, immaculately dressed in grey suit and broad-brimmed hat, sat astride a roan as he glared down at the scene before him.

Julie recognized her rescuer immediately: Crichton Randolph, the lawyer who had shown great interest in her.

'Get down from there, both of you.'

Neither Cas nor Rufus obeyed, but they released their grip and Julie was able to wriggle back and sit up. Without thinking she straightened her dress and rearranged her hair.

Rufus twisted his lips in a snarl. 'Goddamn it!' he shouted. 'Yer interferin' where ya shouldn't. If ya know what's good for ya you'll ride on.'

The lawyer shook his head. 'I know you. You're nothing but trouble. I'll have both of you driven out of town. This sort of behaviour cannot be tolerated.'

The men stood up, neither appearing to be intimidated. 'An' just what're ya intendin' to do about it now?' Cas asked, his hand dropping down to his holster. 'An' you not even wearin' a gun.'

Rufus had already drawn his Colt. 'You'll do nothing,' he sneered, 'long as I got this gun on ya.'

'I'm not carryin', as you can see,' Crichton said. 'But I can still give you the whipping of your lives.' His right hand grasped the leather handle of a rawhide whip. The whip snaked out, and with great accuracy took the gun from Rufus's hand. 'Now, git mounted and high-tail it outa here.'

'Damn you!' Rufus yelled.

Cas went to draw his own weapon but his hand clutched at an empty holster.

For the space of a breath nobody moved. Then, 'Do as he tells you!'

During the heated exchange the men had forgotten Julie's presence. Now they whirled to see her holding Cas's Colt, firm and steady in both hands. They didn't miss the fact that the hammer was already cocked, ready for firing.

Cas and Rufus stood open-mouthed. 'Well, I'll be damned,' Rufus growled. 'D'ya know how to use that thing?'

By way of a reply Julie fired a shot into the air, the sudden sound causing the bay to shy. Julie staggered, but retained her hold on the gun, thumbing back the hammer for a second shot if needed.

'Goddamn! A woman with a gun! How dangerous is that?'

Cas didn't wait for an answer. He sprang at Julie and she stepped back as far as she could go, her finger jerking on the trigger.

Rufus yelled and clutched at his arm as the slug bit deep.

'Best do what I told you,' the lawyer said, grinning broadly, 'afore she takes it into her head to fire again. Don't wanna cart you home horizontal.'

Reluctantly, Rufus and Cas stepped down from the buckboard, their faces twisted in anger. 'This ain't finished,' Rufus shouted, glaring up at Julie, who had been as shocked as they were at the turn of events. Her legs were trembling and the Colt felt heavy in her hands.

She watched as the two men remounted and turned their horses towards town. The lawyer said something to Cas that Julie couldn't hear. Whatever it was, the two riders spurred their horses and rode away fast without another word.

'I'm mighty grateful to you,' she said as she eased her way on to the seat of the buckboard. 'That was a brave thing you did, challenging those two thugs, and you not even wearing a gun. Where did you learn that trick with a whip?'

Crichton slid from the saddle. 'I know many tricks. Learned them from my pa when I was young. Snakes like those two only know about guns; think they're the answer to everything.'

He reached up to take her outstretched hands and helped her down. 'You're shaking,' he said, and pulled her gently into his arms. They remained like that for several minutes until Julie pulled back. 'I was scared,' she admitted. 'If you hadn't happened along . . . '

'But I did,' Crichton told her, gently. 'Let us thank the Good Lord for that. And,' he added, 'you had the presence of mind to snatch Cas's gun. You're a young woman a man would be proud to have at his side.'

'Thank you,' Julie said. 'Now I must go and finish my duties or I'll be in trouble at home.'

'Well, I'm going to see you safely into town and back home again, an' I won't take no for an answer. You never know what those two young thugs have in their minds.' He hitched his horse to the back of the buckboard, and he and Julie climbed back on to the seat. He took the reins as Julie sat beside him.

They rode in silence for a while. Julie felt she had nothing left to say, but became aware that Crichton was weighing up his words. She waited, relieved that she was not alone.

At last Crichton took a deep breath. 'Julie, this may not be the right time, but the matter has taken on an urgency that causes me to speak my mind.' He waited, but when Julie gave no help he continued, 'Urgent, because very shortly my business will take me away from Redstone Creek, and I need an answer from you to the question I have asked before.'

Julie, still recovering from the shock of the attack, did not feel ready to give him the reply he needed. 'Leaving town?' she asked. 'How long for?'

'A long time. Probably for ever.' Thinking it unwise to have admitted that, he added, 'Nobody knows that but you. Please keep it to yourself.'

'Of course, Crichton. Where're you going?'

'East. As far away from here as possible.'

'Oh.'

'America's a big place. Mebbe settle in a large town or city somewhere. I don't want to go alone. There's a new life waiting for both of us as husband and wife in the East if you'll just say yes. You've had some time to think over my proposal. I was sorta hoping you'd made up your mind.'

Julie had long dreamed of love, of romance, of settling down and living peacefully and happily, and eventually producing a family of her own. Is that what Crichton was offering her? He professed to love her and he was, without doubt, a man of substance. He could take her away from her adoptive parents, who had treated her as a servant. He had promised her a better life and had made his feelings plain.

And he had now proved himself to be a courageous man.

She had given much thought to his proposals and had tried to analyze her own feelings when she was alone in her bed at night. She could not feel the love for him that she wanted. Was admiration enough?

'Yes,' she said. 'I'd be honoured to marry you.'

He put his arms around her and briefly kissed her on the cheek. 'I'm a happy man,' he said. 'Now, I'm gonna stay with you while you finish your business in town, then see you safely back to the farm. Tomorrow I'll call on you and take you back with me. You'll stay in the hotel here that night and we can get married.'

★ ★ ★

The speed of events made Julie's head whirl. What had she done? She was going to be a married woman with a husband older by thirteen years. What did she know about him? She responded automatically to his embrace, but withdrew slightly when he leaned forward to kiss her on the mouth.

As he had promised he stayed with her while she completed the business she had set out for. At Julie's insistence they paid a visit to Marshal Scott McQuade.

'We have to tell him what's been going on,' she said. 'I'm not the only young woman who travels alone, and those two men need to be kept in check.'

Crichton attempted to persuade her against the idea. 'Marshal McQuade's not a man of action. I have some influence in this town,' he told her. 'I'll see to it that this sort of thing is stopped.'

Julie was about to agree when the marshal stepped out in front of them, and Crichton felt obliged to relate the incident to him. The lawman was a tall, bewhiskered man around middle age. It was hard to tell exactly how old he might be. Behind the facial hair his expression was one of perpetual surprise.

'I'll keep my eyes open,' the marshal said. 'There's not much else I kin do 'less you wanna make out a complaint agin 'em.' He looked questioningly at Julie. 'Though I wouldn't advise that. They're liable to take that as a challenge.'

Julie glanced at Crichton, who nodded his agreement.

'The marshal's right. They've had enough of a fright with Rufus taking a slug. Let me speak to them. I'll put the fear of God into 'em.'

The marshal was clearly relieved. 'Best way,' he said. 'Will you see the young lady home, Crichton?'

'Already taken care of,' the lawyer said, and turned to go.

'By the way,' the marshal called. 'How're negotiations about the land rights goin' with the Railroad Company? Bin some time now since we heard.'

Crichton stood still and hesitated

briefly before replying. 'Fine, Scott. Jus' dandy. Deal should be settled in a day or so. Then it's just a question of signin' on the dotted line. I'll let ya know. Meantime it's best if we keep our mouths shut 'til the money's paid over.'

They climbed up on the buckboard and urged the horse forward, speaking very little until they were well clear of the town.

At length, Julie asked, 'What was that about the railroad?'

'Nothing to worry your pretty head about,' Crichton said. 'It'll put money in our pockets, that's all you need to know jus' now.'

As they came in sight of Julie's home they stopped the buckboard. This time Julie responded as Crichton leaned over and kissed her.

He untied his own mount. 'You'll be safe from here,' he said. 'Tomorrow I'll call for you.'

She smiled and set the buckboard rolling down the slope towards the house. She knew she would be in trouble for being late, but somehow that thought failed to concern her.

★ ★ ★

Crichton watched her go, wheeling the roan and setting it into a smart canter while his mind raced. Events had progressed faster than he had anticipated.

As he had left the marshal he had felt the lawman's eyes on his back, and when he turned he thought he had seen a puzzled look on his face. He persuaded himself that he'd been mistaken by a trick of the light, but if the marshal had started to harbour suspicions others would follow. It was time to get things moving.

He was pleased with himself as he rode, the movement of the animal beneath him providing a pleasing rhythm to his thoughts. The fact that he would have to leave Redstone Creek, never to return, did not bother him. He would be a very rich man and he would have with him a young, beautiful wife. What more could a man want?

But first there were some loose ends to clear up.

When he reached town he immediately made for the saloon where he knew Cas and Rufus would be waiting for him. In fact they could be found there at most times of the day and would probably have consumed a considerable amount of whiskey or beer. They were partial to both.

He hitched his horse to the rail and pushed through the batwings. The two men were seated at a corner table. Each had a glass set in front of them. Crichton suppressed a grin as he noticed that Rufus had one arm resting in a sling, and that Cas had his arm around the waist of a young lady of uncertain age and morals.

The lawyer went to the bar and ordered two whiskeys, which he carried over to the men. They looked up and scowled as he strode towards them. He placed the drink on the table and drew up another chair.

''Bout time,' Rufus growled.

Crichton raised his eyebrows. 'Well, I'm here now. Anyway, seems to me you've found something to keep you from being bored.' He turned to the dove. 'Could you detach yourself for a moment while I have a word with these two' — he hesitated — 'with these gentlemen?'

The lady needed no further encouragement. When she was out of earshot, Crichton said, 'You went too far. You didn't stick to our bargain.'

'We was havin' fun.'

'That wasn't what we agreed.'

'She's a good-looking gal,' Cas said. 'What did ya expect?'

'I expected you to do what I asked.'

'We gave her a scare,' Cas said. 'That's what ya wanted.'

Crichton grunted. 'OK, what's done is done an' no harm came to her. If it had you'd both be dead men.'

'You owe us,' Rufus snarled.

Crichton ran his hand over his chin.

'Right. I'm gonna settle up with you, after which no one is to know what went on between us. Is that agreed?'

Both men nodded.

'Hundred dollars each. That was the arrangement.' He unfolded the bills from his wallet and slid them across the table.

He made to rise but Cas laid a hand on his shoulder. 'The price went up.'

The lawyer's eyes blazed as anger welled up. 'What in tarnation for? Looked to me as if you were enjoying yourselves too much.'

Rufus patted his injured arm. 'That's what fer,' he grated. 'Ya didn't warn us she was likely to fight back. An' then there's the matter of that whip o' yourn.' He pointed to the red weal across the back of his hand where the leather had bitten. 'Where'd ya learn to do that?'

'I have many talents, as you'll find out if you ever try to cross me. How much d'ya reckon you're worth?'

Rufus grinned. 'Another hunnerd. I

didn't reckon on gettin' injured.'

Crichton took a deep breath. He was going to have to do something about these two. 'Right, three hundred. Our agreement still stands. Otherwise you'll find yourselves heading for Boot Hill.' He laid the notes down, rose and strode away without looking back.

3

In the town of Elsewhere four young men, Saul, Seth, Brett and Hal, sat at a corner table of the Silver Spur saloon. They were silent, each contemplating their empty glasses.

'What're we gonna do fer cash?' Seth asked.

Brett upended the empty bottle and a few drops fell into his glass. 'We could git work,' he suggested without much conviction. 'I hear they're lookin' fer wranglers.' He stopped, as his companions stared at him with open mouths.

'We're not built fer work like that,' Seth said. 'I hear ya kin get yersel' killed doin' that sorta thing.'

'There's easier pickin's than work,' Saul said. 'My pa's got some savin's stashed away.'

'How much?'

'Coupla hunnerd.'

None of them spoke while they digested that information.

'Not gonna keep us in whiskey fer long,' Seth complained. 'We need somethin' bigger than that.'

'Like holdin' up a stagecoach or robbin' a bank?' Saul demanded.

'Yeah, somethin' like that.'

Brett laughed. 'I don't figure on findin' myself in jail.'

'No chance if'n they don't catch us,' Saul said, the light of enthusiasm in his eyes.

'Yer serious?' Seth asked.

'Guess I am,' Saul said, although he sounded surprised at his own suggestion. 'Reckon that calls fer another drink.' He rose and sauntered over to the bar. 'Another bottle!' he demanded.

The barkeep shook his head. 'Sorry, Saul. 'Less yer got some money to back that up.'

'I'm good fer another,' Saul snarled. 'I'll pay ya tomorrow.'

The barkeep was used to dealing with difficult customers. 'Take my advice,' he said, reasonably. 'Go make yersel' an honest dollar, then come back an' I'll serve ya. Go home an' take yer pards with ya afore ya git into trouble. Get some work. There's plenty of dollars to be had if yer prepared to work fer 'em.'

Saul backed off reluctantly and went back to his table where the four men sat for a while gazing at their empty glasses and eyeing the saloon girls longingly.

'We're gonna do it!' Saul announced at last, banging his fist on the table. 'Not a stagecoach right off. We'll start with somethin' small. In an' out quick.'

Slowly the notion took root in their minds. This idea was something new. They had never shrunk from stealing, robbing, grabbing anything they could get their hands on, but becoming outlaws smacked of danger. And with danger came excitement.

'When do we start?' Seth asked, as if the decision had already been made.

'Are we all agreed?' Saul's confident

smile showed he had already established himself as the leader of an outlaw gang. He waited for their agreement, then continued, 'Way I see it we ride out singly afore sunup an' meet at Conway's Bluff. We go fer a place where there might be pickin's, then we go in quick, help oursel's an' git out. We git back to town after dark an' meet up here as if nothin's happened.'

There were vigorous nods from his companions.

*   *   *

Brad loved his new life, although, even after twelve years, he still missed his sister. All the enquiries he had made had turned up no information of where she had been taken or where she now was. He hoped she had been as happy as he was.

The time he had lived with his new family had seen him develop into a strong and able young man. He had learned early on to avoid confrontation with Saul, although that had not always been possible, and he had taken and given punishment on a number of occasions.

Fortunately, as the years had gone by, Saul had spent more and more time away from the house, allowing Brad to take over his responsibilities. He learned fast, developing a close companionship with Kate, who had grown up into an attractive young woman. They had found a mutual trust and liking for each other that had grown with the years.

When Saul made an appearance it was usually to rob his parents of whatever he could get his hands on. Sam and Sadie accepted this with resignation, and came to rely on their new son as part of the family, although never formally adopting him.

'Brad,' Sam called. 'I need you to take the wagon into Elsewhere and git some more provisions. I'll give you a list. An' call in at the livery an' git a couple o' these hosses reshod. Tell Joe to hurry it along. You might find him in the saloon. He needs a reminder now and again that some o' us have deadlines.'

The sun was at its highest as Brad drove the wagon through the gates. Sweat beaded his brow under the broad brim of his Stetson. The ride into town was dusty and hot, and by the time he had loaded up at the store the heat had not abated. He had another hour to wait before the two horses at the livery were ready. And his throat was parched.

He allowed his own horses to drink, then he hitched the wagon under the shade of some trees and made his way to the best saloon in town, the Silver Spur. He shouldered the batwings and stood as his eyes adjusted.

There were a few men standing at the long, polished bar who had found it necessary to slake their thirst. The large mirror gave the impression that the room was more spacious than it really was.

'Look who's jest come in.' Saul's taunting voice met him almost immediately. 'If it ain't the rat from the big city!'

Saul had never let Brad forget that he had been born in a city. It didn't worry him overmuch, except that he knew Saul said it to needle him into a fight.

Brad sauntered up to the bar. In the mirror he could see that Saul was seated at a table by the wall. With him were three young men, all with the same appearance of worthlessness.

Brad ignored the taunt and ordered a cold beer from the barkeep, a powerfully built man wearing a clean white apron over a check shirt, who was clearly displeased with the group.

Brad gestured with his thumb. 'How long's he bin here?'

'Hour or so,' the barkeep said. 'Prob'ly bin turned outa the Longhorn. Won't last long here neither if'n they don't behave theirselves. Good fer business, only if they've got cash an' stay quiet. Trouble is, their pockets are empty an' they can't keep their mouths shut.'

As if to prove the point Saul banged his glass on the table. 'Another round, Harry,' he shouted. 'An' we'd like it afore ya serve my esteemed brother.' The four men thought this was hilariously funny.

'Best see to 'em,' Brad said.

'Nosir!' The barkeep took his time to pour a glass of beer and push it across the counter. 'I'll serve 'em when I'm good an' ready an' not a second before.'

A sudden scraping of chair legs on the wooden floor alerted Brad to the possibility that Saul had not taken the delay well. He swung round as the four men swaggered towards the bar and pushed their way through until they had encircled Brad.

Saul reached across the counter, grabbed the barkeep by his shirt and pulled him so that their faces were close. 'I told ya we were ready fer a refill,' he snarled.

Harry didn't flinch, though his face

was colouring in anger. It didn't appear as if he thought there was anything here he couldn't handle. 'I told ya earlier, no cash, no liquor,' he said quietly. 'I'm not looking fer trouble, but if'n ya don't let go of my shirt you'll not have much use of that hand fer a while.'

Saul relaxed his grip. 'I ain't done with ya yet,' he mumbled, then muscled in on Brad's space, trying to push him along the bar. As Brad stood his ground he picked up Brad's glass and emptied the contents on to the polished wood. 'Time ya learned yer manners.'

Brad reacted quickly as he felt strong hands clutching at his arms. He wrenched free and thrust his elbow sharply back. He was rewarded with a satisfying grunt of pain.

Saul grinned and turned his full attention on to his brother. 'Reckon ya should apologize to the barkeep fer spilling yer beer,' he sniggered.

Brad stopped struggling and became aware that the room was falling silent as men realized that there was a fight in the air. He signalled to Harry, who was reaching under the counter, that this was his problem and he would deal with it.

'Go home, Saul,' he said, mildly. 'Your pa could do with some help around the place.' He realized that he was in no position to fight the four men even if he had been wearing a gun. His best hope to avoid the confrontation was to persuade them that he had no intention of doing so. He stepped back from the bar, pushing the other three men with him.

'I'll go back when I'm ready,' Saul grated. 'Jest remember whose home it is. You ain't permanent there. Time'll come when the farm's mine an' you'll be sent on yer way. I allus figured you'd try to take my place, but it ain't gonna happen.'

Brad shrugged. 'The way you're heading you'll end up on Boot Hill before ya get much older. Same goes fer yer buddies.' He turned to the barkeep, who had finished mopping up the spilled liquid and was standing ready to intervene. 'I'll have that cold beer when ya ready, Sam, an' ya kin pour one fer my friends here.'

Saul wasn't to be put off from what he had started. 'Ya know, I figure ya need to be taught a lesson or two, an' I'm the one to do it.' Brad's grin at this seemed to annoy him. 'I explained to ya when ya first arrived that ya weren't welcome. It's time I sorta reminded ya.'

Brad, aware of the closeness of the other men, said, 'I was jus' seven then, if I recall, an' you were bigger an' stronger than I was. You kin see I've growed up a mite since. Age difference don't mean a thing.'

Saul sneered. 'Ya reckon yer a man now?'

'Man enough not to need the help of three men.'

'I don't need no help. I whipped ya then an' I'll sure whip ya now. You either back away like a mangy cur or you stand up an' face me. Either way you'll be as good as dead.' He signalled

54

to his pals to step away. Other men also moved clear.

Brad bowed to the inevitable. 'So it's a fight yer lookin' fer. P'raps we'd best get this over once an' for all.'

Saul chuckled. 'Suits me.' His eyes swept down to Brad's hips. 'Where's yer gun? Cain't shoot a man who cain't defend hisself.'

'I don't carry,' Brad said. 'Don't see no reason to.' He had to think fast. If he played this wrong he could be dead in the next few minutes. 'Tell ya what. We'll go outside an' settle this man to man. No guns. No knives. A fair fight.'

A cruel sneer spread across Saul's face. 'Reckon ya kin beat me? I seem to recall I've beat ya a few times.' He grinned at his three companions. 'You kin see to it that it's a fair fight.' He slapped his holster, slid the Colt from leather and laid it on the polished wood of the bar. 'I won't be needin' this.'

Without warning he slammed a vicious fist into Brad's solar plexus. Brad doubled up and staggered back, attempting to block the rain of blows that followed.

He recovered quickly and began an attack of his own, gritting his teeth as more of Saul's punches broke through his guard.

By now he was giving as good as he received, and he sensed that Saul's recent lifestyle had softened his body and his muscles. Brad's muscles were hard from work on the farm, but even so Saul had the advantage of size and weight, and his punches were beginning to hurt. Tables were knocked over, chairs sent skidding across the floor.

But Brad's own punches were sinking into flesh and bringing gasps of pain from his opponent. He stepped back. 'Had enough?' he asked. 'I've no wish to do ya harm.'

By way of an answer Saul rushed forward, fists flying. Brad let him come, swayed and ducked, then let loose with a sledgehammer blow to Saul's chest followed by an uppercut to the jaw.

Saul's head snapped back, and for a

moment he stood without moving, then slowly buckled at the knees until he was kneeling on the wood floor, giving the appearance that he was in prayer. Praying was the last thing on his mind as a torrent of profanities poured from his lips.

Brad stood with his arms loosely at his side, then held out a hand to help his brother up. But Saul was having nothing to do with it. He struggled to his feet, his right hand snaking down to his hip, only to find an empty holster.

'Goddamn it!' he snarled. 'I'm gonna kill ya.'

Brad shrugged, turned, and pushed his way through the spectators towards the batwings. As he went out he looked back in time to see that Saul had swept his gun from the bar and was bringing it to bear.

4

Crichton Randolph smiled as he approached the farm. He wondered if Julie had broken the news to her adoptive parents of her forthcoming marriage. He doubted they would be pleased.

'A welcome visit,' Joe Sawyer said as Crichton stepped down from his horse. 'We was sorta expectin' to hear from you about how the plans fer the rail line're goin'. I gotta lot o' money tied up in them Land Right shares.'

'Yeah, the spur line,' Crichton said, while he thought of an appropriate reply. 'Should have something definite in a few days.' He smiled reassuringly. 'These things take time. Afore long those shares'll be worth a load o' dollars. Tell you what, I'm prepared to buy those shares off'n you for the price you paid for 'em. Cash. Good profit for me.'

Avarice glowed in the farmer's eyes. 'Only askin'. I kin wait.'

The lawyer's smile was even broader. How easy it was to dupe greedy men out of their money.

The man seemed to accept his answer but looked questioningly at the sorrel that Crichton was trailing. 'What's the spare horse fer?'

'It's for Julie,' Crichton said, and watched the look of surprise on the man's face. 'I've come for her.'

Joe raised his eyebrows. 'Julie?' he repeated. 'Is she in trouble or something?'

'Nope, not s'far as I know. She's gonna leave here. I've come to take her away.'

The farmer's features registered surprise, anger and determination in swift succession. 'She ain't doin' nothin' o' the sort!'

'That's for Julie to decide, don't you think?'

'Why's she wantin' to leave? She come into money? We've bin meanin' to adopt her legal but never got round to it. I was sayin' only yesterday — '

The lawyer held up his hand. 'Nothing to do with that. I reckoned she might've told you. Is she around somewhere?'

'Doggone it,' the farmer said. 'She'll be shirkin' her duties, I 'spect. I'll find the stupid girl. But you're not takin' her anywhere. She stays here. We've given her everythin', spent a lotta money bringin' her up. Without us where would she be?'

He stormed off, and Crichton waited.

When Julie appeared, urged on by her pa, her face was flushed as if she had been hard at work. Crichton put another interpretation on it: anger, perhaps, or excitement. He took her arm before she could say anything, and pulled her close.

Joe stood with his mouth open in bewilderment. 'What's the meanin' of this?' he demanded.

Crichton ignored him. 'I reckon you didn't tell them.' He jerked his thumb in the direction of her pa.

Julie shook her head. 'Never seemed the right time.'

'Well, he knows now. Ready to go?' he asked.

There was no hesitation in Julie's response. 'Yes, Crichton, I am. I've got a few things packed.'

Crichton kissed her on the cheek. 'Go get them, while I explain everything.'

She'd taken only one step when Joe grabbed her arm. 'No you don't!' he roared. 'If yer leavin' yer goin' with nothin'. Same as ya come with.'

Crichton's gaze turned icy. 'Let her go!' He spoke softly, but the farmer got the message and released his grip.

'Julie has no loyalty to you. She owes you nothing. If there's any debt to be paid it's you should be doing the paying. She's of age to make up her own mind where her future lies. You kin go an' find yourselves another slave.'

He looked at his future bride. 'You won't need to bring much with you,' he told her. 'We'll get everything you need from the stores in town. This is a new beginning. For both of us.'

Julie raised her face to the lawyer. 'They gave me a home,' she told him. 'I can't leave without saying goodbye to Ma.'

'Right, Julie,' Crichton said. 'But remember they worked you hard. You gave as well as received. You owe them nothing. I'll wait here while you go and do what you have to.'

As Julie ran off Joe yelled, 'You can't do this!'

'Already done.'

Julie returned quickly, clutching a bundle of items in a calico bag. Crichton took it from her and hooked it on to the cantle of his mount. 'Time to go.'

They both stepped in the saddles and, without another word, turned their horses towards Redstone Creek.

Cries of, 'Ungrateful Jezebel!' followed them until they were out of earshot.

They rode without speaking, each busy with their own thoughts. Crichton was the first to break the silence. 'I've made arrangements for tomorrow for our wedding with the preacher.'

'It's so sudden,' Julie said. 'I've only just got used to the idea.'

'Yeah. Long as we're both of a mind I reckoned it was best to go ahead as soon as possible. We'll be husband and wife. Does that idea please you?'

'Of course it does, Crichton.'

Julie's response, sounding genuine, encouraged Crichton to continue. 'That's all I wanted to hear. Something's happened to cause me to hasten our plans for going east an' I wanted us to get married before we set off.' He thought it best not to expand on that.

On reaching town they busied themselves choosing clothes for Julie and installing her into the best hotel Redstone Creek could offer.

'Buy whatever else you think necessary to get yerself ready fer the wedding,' Crichton told her. 'Don't concern yerself with what it costs. Tell the store owners to send me the bill. They know I'm good for the money. I'll come and visit you later on this evening and we'll have dinner together. Meantime I've some business to see to.' He kissed her on the mouth and was pleased with the way she responded.

He left her and took both horses to the livery where he left instructions for them to be given the very best of treatment, although he didn't say that he would have no further use for them. Redstone Creek would not be seeing him again once he and Julie set off.

The first part of their journey, taking them to Elsewhere, would be by stage. Julie had made it clear that she would prefer that mode of travel, perhaps recalling her first unhappy journey. Crichton, although preferring the train, had raised no objection to this.

He made his way to his office where he spent several hours going through old documents. He checked the safe and stuffed some old papers roughly into a bag, to be burned later. Charles Hinckley might not be easily fooled but it only needed a few moments to divert his attention, giving Crichton the opportunity to do what he had to.

Lastly, he again checked the little Deringer.

At the back of the livery, away from the glare of the kerosene lamps lining the main drag, he found Charles waiting, concealed by a wooden fence.

'I'm alone,' Crichton called softly. 'Let's make this quick.'

Charles came out from cover, clearly nervous. 'Suits me. Have ya got it?'

Crichton waved the bag in front of him. 'All there as promised,' he lied. 'This is the last time we meet. Understood?'

'Give me what ya owe me an' ya'll never see me agin.' Charles stretched out his hand for the package.

The lawyer held it out, then withdrew it swiftly. 'An' not a word will pass your lips about our little arrangement?'

'I'm in this as deep as you,' Charles said, impatiently.

That answer was not as reassuring as Crichton would have liked. With his fingers curled round the small gun in his coat pocket, he hesitated. Not that he had any compunction in shooting this man, but he wondered whether the killing could possibly be traced back to him. Their business relationship was probably no great secret, and someone might have seen Charles come to his office earlier.

Dammit, there was a lot at stake.

'You certain no one saw you visit me today?'

Charles's impatience was rising. 'No! Nobody. Are ya gonna give me that or not?' While his left hand was waiting for the package, his right hand dropped alarmingly towards his holster.

It was now or never. Crichton appeared to accept what Charles was saying. 'All right. We understand each other.' He reached into his coat pocket for the small gun, withdrew it and held the barrel against the other man's chest. He saw the sudden panic in Charles's eyes just before he pulled the trigger. The lead easily found its target.

'Nope, I don't reckon on you ever seeing me again,' he said, as Charles Hinckley's heart stopped beating and its owner sank to the ground. 'Nor anyone else, neither.'

The sound of the explosion of the little gun was surprisingly loud in the silence. Crichton stood still and listened, half expecting to hear running footsteps.

But there was nothing and, with a disdainful glance at the prostrate figure, he pocketed the small gun and made his way back to his office, using the back lots to avoid any chance of being seen.

He was looking forward to a very romantic meal.

He was annoyed, therefore, when he noticed Cas and Rufus approaching the table where he and Julie were seated. He tried to ignore them, but when they stood silently at his elbow he looked up with anger in his eyes.

'Can't you see we're eating?' he asked. 'If you want to talk to me I'll be in my office tomorrow morning.'

'Sorry to trouble ya,' Cas said. 'But we reckoned ya wouldn't mind helpin' us out.' He leered at Julie. 'P'raps we kin get to know each other better later.'

With an apologetic glance at Julie the lawyer shoved his chair back and stood up. 'Helping you out? What in tarnation is that s'posed to mean?'

'We need the money ya owe us.' Cas smirked.

Crichton thought he knew what was in their minds, but he asked, 'And just why do I owe you anything?'

'That little job we did fer ya,' Rufus told him.

Crichton took hold of their elbows and led them away where they couldn't be overheard. 'I paid you for that.'

'That was jus' the deposit,' Rufus said. Then suddenly, 'An' we bumped into Charles Hinckley a while ago.'

Crichton's expression didn't change but his stomach lurched. 'What's that got to do with me?'

'He's dead. We was wonderin' who might've seen him outa this world.'

Crichton couldn't be sure whether they knew or were just guessing. Either way he was prepared to pay them because, like Charles Hinckley, they were not going to live long enough to enjoy it. 'How much?'

'Another coupla hunnerd each'll do fer now.'

He reached into his pocket and handed over two hundred-dollar bills. 'That's all you're going to get,' he grated. 'Now get out of here or you'll be giving the hotel a bad name.'

The two men grinned and glanced across at Julie. 'Good-lookin' gal you got there,' Cas said. They turned and left, leaving Crichton with his decision already made. He knew a man who would dispose of Cas and Rufus for maybe two or three hundred dollars. It would be money well spent.

He went back to his meal, relaxed and smiling. 'Sorry, my dear,' he said as he sat down. 'In my business it's necessary to have dealings with all sorts of people, some good and some bad. And those men, as you've already experienced, are two of the very worst. It won't happen again.'

5

Eighty miles away in the town of Elsewhere, at the Silver Spur saloon, Brad wondered whether he was going to be shot in the back by his adopted brother. He couldn't afford to wait to find out. He ducked, shouldered the batwings and stepped swiftly outside.

There he immediately concealed himself to one side, flattening himself against the wall as he heard Saul's heavy footsteps following him.

Saul, gun in hand, hurled himself through the doors, then stood uncertainly, searching for his target. He whirled as Brad's hand shot out, grasped Saul's gun hand and twisted. The Colt fell on to the wooden boardwalk, but Brad knew he was still in trouble as Saul's buddies poured out of the saloon. They seemed to have one thing on their minds as their hands dropped to their holsters.

The odds were too heavy. Brad stooped, quickly retrieved the fallen weapon and thumbed the hammer.

'Stop!' he ordered. 'I'm leavin'. This has gone far enough. Keep yer hands clear of yer guns an' ya won't get hurt.'

The men stopped in the act of clearing leather and Brad took a step back. But that was as far as he got as Saul rushed at him with a growl of fury. Brad, with no thought of pulling the trigger, had no chance to avoid the heavy contact, and both men were propelled by Saul's momentum down the steps and into the street.

As Brad fell his finger twitched and the roar of the .45 drowned all other sounds. In the brief silence that followed a yell came from one of the men.

'Hal's bin hit!'

Brad and Saul clambered to their feet. 'Ya've shot one o' my friends,' Saul snarled.

Brad was gazing down at the gun still

clutched in his hand, then at the man who had collapsed against the wall of the saloon and who was not moving.

'He's dead,' someone said. 'Fetch the sheriff.'

But there was no need, for the sheriff had already been informed of the disturbance in the saloon and the sound of the shot caused him to hasten his footsteps. He took in the scene at a glance.

'I'll take that!' he said, as he levered the Colt from Brad's grip.

Miles Pitcher was a lawman who took his job seriously. A thin, wiry man, but well muscled, he made his mind up quickly and was not disposed to listen to arguments. He had been appointed to his position five years ago in the expectation that he could easily be manipulated by the town council. As it was, he had proved himself to be a man who did things his way.

He glared around, bent to examine the dead man and straightened with a shrug of his shoulders. 'Anyone tell me what happened here?'

Saul and his buddies were only too happy to oblige, while, under the glare of their threatening gaze, other onlookers slunk away. Their version of events, however, bore only a passing resemblance to the truth.

'An' what've you gotta say fer yerself?' the sheriff demanded of Brad.

'Self-defence,' Brad told him angrily. 'I was bein' attacked.'

'You seemed to be the only one holding a gun,' the sheriff observed, and then noticed that Brad was not wearing a gunbelt. 'Where'd ya git the weapon?'

Brad pointed to Saul's empty holster, but before he could explain Saul said, 'Yeah, Sheriff, we was havin' a friendly chat, then he made a grab fer my gun, an' before we knew it he took a shot at me.'

'Lucky he missed.'

'Not so lucky fer Hal. Yer kin ask my buddies here. They'll tell you I'm tellin' the truth. It's murder, pure an' simple.' He levelled a finger at Brad. 'You've gotta lock him up 'til he kin feel the rope round his neck.'

The lawman looked at the young men who were still standing outside the batwings, blocking the exit. He raised his eyebrows questioningly.

Saul's cronies nodded. 'It's like he says,' one of them said. 'We was comin' outa the saloon peaceful, mindin' our own business.'

'Yeah, I got the picture.' The sheriff handed Saul's weapon back, then stepped up to Brad. 'Seems a clear case of murder to me,' he said. 'I'm gonna have to put you in one o' my cells while I see if I kin find someone to back up ya story.'

'It didn't happen like he told ya — '

'You kin tell me all that down at the office,' the lawman interrupted. 'Fer now ya comin' with me.' As he said this both the doc and the undertaker arrived.

It did not escape Brad's attention

that Miles Pitcher still had his Colt out of its holster. 'Ya got it wrong,' he said as he was propelled towards the law office.

'Yer Saul's brother of a sorts, ain't ya?'

'He's no kin o' mine,' Brad said hotly. As he glanced behind him he saw the grins of triumph on the faces of Saul and his cronies.

At the law office the sheriff ushered Brad inside. 'Siddown an' behave yerself an' I might not have to shoot ya.' He settled himself into a creaking leather chair and laid his .45 on the desk in front of him. 'Don't git any ideas.' He fired up a thin cigar, his eyes never leaving his prisoner. 'Now, I noticed you ain't carryin' a gun.'

'Nope.'

'I've seen ya with a gun afore now.'

'Yep.'

'Have to use it often?'

'Only as often as I need to,' Brad said.

'An' how often might that be?'

'Cain't recall the last time. Mebbe it was last week when I was forced to kill a rattler.'

'Ever used it on anyone?'

'Nope.'

'Yet ya used one today. Who were ya aimin' at?'

Brad didn't like the way the conversation was going. He wasn't a killer. Not even of rattlesnakes unless it was necessary. Until now he hadn't even come close to killing a human being. He doubted he could do it.

'Listen, Sheriff. My, er, brother an' his pards were gonna kill me. Saul's gone bad, but it weren't my intention to shoot him, nor any of 'em. We fought 'cos he reckons he's gotta score to settle.'

The sheriff remained silent as he mulled over what he'd been told. 'Well, I've half a mind to believe ya, but from what I saw you were the only one holding the gun an' ya shot an' killed a man. Like I said, it's my duty to lock you up until I kin investigate further.'

He picked up the Colt and gestured towards the cells.

'I gotta wagon full o' provisions an' hosses to see to.'

'Leave 'em to me. I'll get 'em taken to the livery.'

'I gotta get word to Pa.'

'I'll see to that, too. I'm not havin' a killer run around loose.'

Brad shrugged. He had little choice. He felt confident that the sheriff would be as good as his word and would do everything he could to find out the truth. Also his pa would not let him rot in jail.

'You're wrong,' he said. 'I'm not the one should be locked up.' Nevertheless he allowed himself to be directed to the cells.

'Yeah. I've had folk tell me that afore.'

'Yer makin' a bad mistake, Sheriff.'

As the metal door clanged shut he swore under his breath.

★ ★ ★

After the dead body of Hal had been taken away Saul and the remaining two wasters, Seth and Brett, swaggered back into the saloon. Saul made a show of easing his Colt in its holster and glaring at anyone who dared to raise their eyes in judgement of him.

'Ya all saw it! Plain case o' murder.'

He knew that, although the men in the saloon had witnessed the beginning of the argument, nobody had seen the actual shooting. He was going to make damned sure that there would be no one foolish enough to speak up against him.

He strode up to the bar. 'Reckon we need a drink to settle our nerves,' he told the barkeep. 'Three whiskeys. I'll pay ya tomorrow.'

Harry was about to refuse but, looking around the room and finding no ready support, he filled three glasses and pushed them across. 'Sure. Ya pay tomorrow or ya'll not be welcome in this saloon agin.'

79

Saul carried the drinks to a vacant table. When the men were seated he leaned forward. 'Things are goin' our way,' he said. 'Tomorrow we make our first raid as the . . . ' he hesitated, 'as the Coyote Gang.' He liked the sound of that.

He waited for the reaction, but drew back his lips in contempt when it was less than enthusiastic. 'C'mon, I feel good about this. If any of ya don't wanna be part of this ya'd better say so now.'

No one moved. 'Yep,' he continued. 'Like we agreed, we meet at Conway's Bluff afore sunup tomorrow. Make sure yer not seen as ya leave town, an' bring somethin' you kin tie over yer faces. We don't wanna be recognized.'

Seth nodded. 'What then?' he asked.

'What then? We get us some easy dollars, that's what. Leave that side o' the business to me.'

He knew where the first raid of the Coyote Gang was going to take place. He had already scouted the area and had settled on a small, remote home-stead, some two hours' ride away. The pickings would not be rich, although he hoped they might be easy; a test for the gang to see how well they could operate. It would be easy to ride in hard, throw a scare into whoever was about at the time and then disappear.

Saul grinned at the members of his gang, feeling confident in his new role as leader. 'Trust me. This'll be our first raid jus' to see how it goes. I know what I'm doing.'

This was to be a trial run, a practice for bigger and better things to come. Excitement brewed in his mind.

The newly formed Coyote Gang drained their glasses, rose and went out into the late sun.

6

Kate was helping her ma with the household chores when a boy of about fourteen years of age rode into the yard. He had pushed his horse hard.

'I know him,' Kate said. 'It's Tom, who helps out at the livery. Wonder what he wants?' She removed her calico apron as she ran out into the fading light. 'Hi, Tom. What brings you here so late?'

'Message fer ya pa from the sheriff,' Tom said as he slid from his pony's back.

'How serious?'

'Very serious, I think,' the boy said. 'Ya brother's bin put in jail.'

'Saul? I'm not surprised. What's he s'posed to've done?'

'Not Saul. It's Brad.'

Kate opened her mouth, then closed it again. 'I'll fetch Pa. Better come in.

Ma'll have some soup on the stove. I'll see to the mare.'

After a few minutes Sam Finnan came at the run. 'What's this about Brad?' he demanded.

'Sorry, Mr Finnan,' Tom said. 'Message from the sheriff. Brad's bin arrested fer murder.'

In the silence that followed this announcement Sadie Finnan gasped and turned pale. Sam let out his breath. Tom could be heard sucking soup from his spoon until he became aware that that was where the noise was coming from.

'Murder? Who, goddamn it? Sorry, son, it's come as something of a shock. What else d'ya know?'

'Only that they carted a body away from the saloon. That's all I saw.'

'Right, Tom, thanks for bringing the message. You'd be wise to get back to town while there's still some light. Here.' He reached down a tin box and took out a coin which he laid into the boy's hand. 'Ya did well.'

The boy looked down at the silver and smiled his thanks. 'Din't mind. Better'n work. Good soup, ma'am.' He remounted his pony and urged it back the way he had come.

They watched as he rode away. 'What d'ya make of that?' Sam said. 'Brad doesn't even wear a gun, an' sure as hell he wouldn't kill anyone.'

'Reckon the sheriff's got it wrong?' Kate asked.

'Wouldn't wonder,' Sam observed. 'Looks like I'll need to ride into town. There's gotta be some mistake. Wouldn't've bin surprised if it'd bin Saul.' He stopped himself. 'I've gotta find out the truth an' we've gotta get the stores an' the horses back.'

Kate placed her hand on her pa's arm. 'Don't worry, Pa. Let me go.'

'It's getting late,' Sadie said.

'I'll stay the night with Marylou,' Kate reassured her. 'She'll give me some supper. I'll ride back and let you know soon's I can.'

Her pa seemed happy to accept this

suggestion. 'Best git goin'', then. First, see Brad an' get the story from him. Mebbe git him outa jail. Then git the hosses and wagon back here.'

Kate hastened to saddle her favourite mare, Betsy. She was pleased her pa had raised no objections and she looked forward to the ride.

There was another reason she had offered to go. For some time she had felt a growing awareness that Brad's presence at the farm had become important to her, and she was keen to discover what sort of trouble he had got himself into and to help if she could.

As she rode at a fast pace towards town with the breeze cooling her face and her hair flowing out from her head, her belief grew that Saul had something to do with Brad's problem. She eased Betsy for a while, but even so the pinto was breathing hard when they reached the sheriff's office.

She hitched the mare to the rail, slid from her back, and ran up the three steps. She knocked and pushed at the door that gave access to the law office. She had expected, or at least hoped, that Miles Pitcher would be on duty. She had briefly met the lawman on two occasions and had formed the impression that he was fair-minded and, although sometimes inflexible, he was also open to reason. All in all, she considered that he would listen to what she had to say.

Her heart sank when she was confronted not by Miles Pitcher but Chas Morgan, the deputy. He was an untidy-looking, gangly man with sharp features below hooded eyes. He was wearing a nasty bruise just under one eye. The silver star pinned to his chest had given him an exaggerated sense of importance. His main aim in life seemed to be to exert his authority over other people.

The deputy had risen to his feet and had a gun in his hand. 'Well, well. This is a real pleasure. Don't very often get such a lovely visitor. Whadya want?'

'I'm visiting your prisoner, not you,'

Kate said, sweetly. 'And you won't have cause to shoot me.'

'No visitors allowed till the judge has bin here,' the deputy growled. His gaze swept up and down Kate's body, finally centring on her eyes. He gave the impression that the beautiful girl who had suddenly appeared before him was an angel come to give him comfort.

Kate retained her calm approach, although his intense stare was making her flesh creep. 'He hasn't been found guilty of any crime yet, has he?'

'S'far as I've bin told it's a clear case o' murder.'

'That doesn't mean he can't speak to someone.'

'I've bin given my orders,' Chas Morgan insisted. 'I'm not s'posed to let anyone in to see the prisoner. What's yer business with him?' He retreated behind the large desk. 'That don't mean ya can't talk to me awhiles. I'll tell ya anythin' ya wanna know.' He gestured to the wooden chair at the other side of the desk, but still held his

Colt which, although not levelled at her, seemed to provide him with confidence.

'I'd feel happier if you'd put your gun down,' Kate said. 'You're not scared of a young woman, are you?'

The deputy reholstered his weapon. 'I'm not scared of nobody. Least of all the likes o' you.'

Kate remained standing. 'I've brought him some food and water,' she said, indicating the small package she was carrying. 'I don't suppose you'd thought to give him any.'

'What's he need that fer? He's gonna hang afore long.' Morgan placed his hands around his throat and pulled his head upwards, mimicking a man hanging on the gallows.

Kate ignored the crude gesture. 'Who says?'

'That's what I've bin told.'

'Well, if he's going to hang there's no reason why he has to go hungry, is there? He might as well hang on a full stomach.'

Morgan had been chewing on something. He wiped his mouth on his sleeve before replying. 'How do I know yer not packing one o' those little hideout guns?'

Kate clenched her fists. 'You can search me if you wish,' she said, knowing that he couldn't, and wouldn't, decline such an offer.

He rose slowly, a leer stretching his lips, and his eyes filling with eager anticipation. 'I'll do just that.'

Kate, recognizing the hidden desire behind the words, flinched as he came closer. If this was what she had to do she would do it. She felt his hands move all over her body, slow and lingering, down her legs, even feeling in her boots. From one of them he removed the slender steel stiletto that she always carried.

'Well, crafty little snake, ain't ya?' He straightend up.

'Now I'd best take a look at what ya got in that package there.'

She released the drawstring and held

the bag out for him to examine the contents. Not satisfied with that, he plunged his hand in and pulled out the bread, cheese and cakes that Kate had packed before leaving. He tore off a hunk of the bread and stuffed it into his mouth.

'Fresh baked,' he said. 'Reckon that's too good fer the prisoner.'

'I can see you're a man who likes the good things in life,' Kate said, trying to keep her expression serious. 'If you let me take this in I'll bring you some next time I visit.'

Apparently content, the deputy said, 'Five minutes, but I'm comin' in with ya, an' if ya so much as . . . ' He left the threat unfinished, but withdrew his .45 again as he ushered her through the dividing door that led to the four cells.

Three cells were unoccupied. In the fourth Brad stood, holding the metal bars, his knuckles white. One cheek was swollen, the flesh turning blue. His eyes opened wide when he saw who his visitor was. He was obviously in pain, but managed to raise a smile through swollen lips.

Chas Morgan leaned against the wall and fired up a cigar.

'What've you done to him?' Kate yelled, her face red with anger.

Chas grinned through uneven teeth. 'Didn't do nothin'. I would've bin happy to oblige, but it was already done.'

She gave him a long stare. 'He needs the doc. Has he been called?'

The deputy shrugged. 'Not my concern.'

'I'll get Doc O'Halloran to look in. You won't find it necessary to search him, I'm sure.'

'Give us some privacy,' Brad said.

Chas Morgan smirked. 'I ain't listenin'. Why'd I wanna do that?'

Kate turned on him. 'There's no call for you to stay. What trouble can I possibly cause? You insisted on searching me so I can't pass your prisoner a weapon, and what we have to say to each other is private. You must realize that, you being so attractive to the ladies.' She winked, hoping he was susceptible to flattery.

'Yeah, I kin understand,' the deputy said. 'You kin have ten minutes. But,' he added with a sly grin, 'I'll have to search ya agin when ya come out. Jest in case.'

Brad was about to say something, but Kate held up her hand. 'Just give us ten minutes alone.'

Chas Morgan retreated to the office and Kate studied Brad's face. 'They treat you badly?'

'I gave as good as I got.'

Her gaze wandered over the bare interior of the cell and then rested on the man in front of her. She tried to hold her emotions in check. This was not the time or place to let him know how she felt. 'Are you hurting?'

'Nope. It's not too bad.'

She nodded her head in the direction of the office. 'And what about food? Have they thought of feeding you?'

'Must've slipped their minds.'

She held out the bag and passed it through the bars of the cell. 'There's water there, too,' she told him. 'Sorry, I couldn't manage anything better.'

'A welcome sight.' He grinned as he examined the contents. 'Both you an' the chow. Thanks fer coming.'

Kate suddenly became aware that Brad was studying her and she found herself blushing. 'Tell me what happened,' she said.

Brad told her exactly how it had been. 'There were a few folk about but they seem intent on mindin' their own business. Nobody saw anything.'

Kate thought for a moment. 'Leave that to me. I know the people of this town and they know me. They'll talk to me.' She lightly touched his fingers as they curled round the bars. 'We'll have you out of here soon,' she told him, and both of them wanted to believe it.

'I'd 'preciate that. Jus' take care. The sheriff might be hunting fer witnesses right now, fer all I know.'

Kate smiled, genuinely for the first

time, a smile that set his pulses racing. 'You can leave Miles Pitcher to me as well.'

Before they could say more to each other Chas Morgan called, 'Yer time's up.' He came through and grabbed her arm.

Kate shrugged him off. 'Be patient!' She turned to Brad. 'I'll be back.' Then she followed Chas Morgan back into the outer office, determined not to allow his hands to touch her again.

'Can I have my knife back, please?' she asked.

The deputy turned the knife over in his hand. 'Sweet little thing, ain't it?'

'I like it.'

'What d'ya carry it fer?'

'Protection,' Kate told him.

He threw it on the desk. 'Take it.'

Without a word she turned and left.

★　★　★

The three members of the Coyote Gang set out well before sunup as arranged, each making his separate way to Conway's Bluff, a high, rocky escarpment where a fast-flowing river swept around a sharp bend and a stand of willow clung to the banks.

This was their first raid and Saul, their self-styled leader, was determined it was going to be successful. Even so he was nervous, this being a big step up from the petty thieving and harassment the group had so far been practising.

They arrived at the meeting point within ten minutes of each other. Saul was first, followed by Brett and, lastly, Seth, who had ridden his mount hard.

Brett was eager to move out. 'Where're we goin'? I don't cotton to this waitin' around.'

Saul grinned. 'Got it all planned out. There's a small homestead a coupla miles away. Isolated. Run by an old man and his wife. There're some hired help but mostly the men are away from the house soon's it's light.

'All we have to do is ride in, put the fear of hell into her, take what we want an' get out. Then we split up an' get back to town. We'll meet up in the Silver Spur as if nothin's happened.'

He turned his horse and led them away. This was to be more than a practice run for the gang; this was a test of his leadership, of his planning and of his skill. He led from the front until the three men reined in their horses on top of a low bluff and watched. They pulled their Stetsons low over their eyes to shield them from the rising sun, still low in the sky. Their hands nervously eased their six-guns from the leather holsters, then they pulled their bandannas up over their faces.

Below them, less than half a mile away, they could make out the small, neat adobe house nestling in the trees and surrounded by a low, white-painted fence. A horse was loose in the tiny corral and a cow grazed contentedly nearby.

At first they saw no other movement. Then a woman in a long blue dress covered by an apron emerged from the door and scattered some food for the chickens scratching in the yard. She looked about her, then went back inside the house.

'Let's git at it!' It was Seth who was keen to start the action. The early rise from his bed had not improved his temper or his patience.

Saul grunted approval. They checked their weapons again and spurred their mounts forward. The horses responded to the silent commands and raced across the intervening land.

At the sound of their approach the woman came out again from the house. For a moment or two she stood on the step, taking in the sight of three men with their faces covered and guns hanging at their hips. She saw this and went back indoors to re-emerge with a double-barrelled shotgun under her arm.

The horses cleared the low fence with ease and came to a stop in front of her, kicking up a cloud of dust that briefly lingered in the still air before settling slowly.

Saul set his eyes on the shotgun, and his hand hovered threateningly over his hip where his Colt snuggled in its holster.

'We'd feel more welcome, ma'am, if you'd lay that weapon on the ground. We don't mean ya no harm.' Beneath his bandanna his mouth stretched into what he imagined might be a reassuring smile.

'You'd be welcome to our home,' the woman said, 'if you'd unbuckle your own gunbelts and step down off them hosses.'

Saul's eyes bored into hers. 'We can't do that, ma'am. I'll ask ya agin. Put the gun down.' His smile faded and his voice took on a harsh tone as he realized that this was not how it was supposed to be.

But the woman was not to be intimidated. She raised the barrel of the shotgun until it pointed directly at him. 'This is my home. Git off our property.'

Without warning Seth drew his pistol and fired. The woman took the slug in the chest, fell to her knees, slowly rolled on to the boarding and lay still. Blood seeped through her thin dress.

Saul swung round in the saddle, his face showing his anger. 'Goddamn it! What fer did ya do that?'

Seth, still holding his gun and clearly shaken by what he had just done, said, 'She was gonna pull the trigger. Can't abide women with guns. Never know what they're gonna do.' He tried to grin.

Saul drew his own Colt and swept it round until it made contact with Seth's head. Seth tumbled from the saddle. 'What the hell?' he slurred through the pain.

'There was to be no shootin'. No killin'. Get over there. See if she's dead.'

Seth raised himself from the dirt and crossed over to examine the woman's body. 'She ain't breathin'.' He leaped into the saddle.

Saul took a quick breath. 'We've gotta get outa here. Now.'

Before any of them could wheel their horses a young man of about eighteen appeared in the doorway, a Winchester held at hip level, the chamber already primed. He was tall and muscular with long, fair hair. He took only a moment to take in what was happening and to look into the eyes of his ma's killers.

As he raised the barrel of his weapon and levelled it at Saul, Seth drew and fired his Colt. The shot ricocheted off the stock of the Winchester and buried itself in the boy's leg. His finger had been curled around the trigger and, as the gun slewed to the side, it sent a slug wide of Saul and into Brett's left shoulder.

'Dammit to hell!' Seth roared. He fired again and shot the boy through the head.

'Let's go!' Saul screamed.

Without waiting to see if his companions were following, he set off at high speed. The others raced after him, fearful that the shots would bring other men running to the scene.

Saul led the way back to Conway's Bluff, where he reined in and slid from the saddle. This had been a disaster. Although he was not averse to violence, and quite enjoyed the thrill of it at times, he had planned for their first raid to be carried out swiftly and cleanly. Now there were two dead bodies and Brett with a slug in his arm.

Saul dismounted, and as Seth brought his horse to a stop he reached up and pulled him to the ground. His fist shot forward and connected with Seth's jaw.

Seth gave out a stunned grunt. 'I saved yer life,' he groaned. 'She was gonna — '

Saul didn't let him finish. He hauled him up by his vest and let fly with another vicious blow to Seth's ribs that sent him reeling. 'Ya've ruined everythin'. We'll have to lie low fer a while. I'd sure as hell like to kill ya, right now, but ya not worth the cost of a slug.'

Brett had joined the group and had

watched the one-sided fight with some interest. He was holding his arm where blood was staining his shirt. 'I got hurt,' he snarled. 'An' none of it were my fault.'

'I b'lieve ya,' Saul admitted. 'Though it sticks in my craw to admit it.' He gave the wound a cursory glance. 'Can't go to the doc with that. We'll have to see to it ourselves.'

'I ain't lettin' either of ya near me,' Brett grated. The others ignored him and, after checking their back trail for any signs of pursuit, they set off back towards town in silence.

7

Crichton Randolph had worked hard to attain everything he could possibly want to make his life pleasant and his future easy: sacks full of dollars, and a beautiful young wife. But folk were becoming impatient for a real return on their investments, the marshal had already revealed his suspicions, and the banker was beginning to ask questions.

'I've gotta conclude negotiations,' he had explained. 'When I come back I'll be able to satisfy all those investors who've had confidence in me.'

The banker had nodded and Crichton smiled reassuringly. It didn't much matter whether he was believed or not. It would soon be too late to do anything about it.

The immediate problem, however, concerned those two no-account wasters, Cas and Rufus. They had to be dealt with before he and Julie left town.

And what of love? Yes, he both loved and desired Julie. Perhaps love was too strong a word for the feelings Julie felt towards him, but he was confident it would develop in time; that the respect that already existed would become stronger once they were married. For Julie the change in her situation had been very sudden, and he had to respect that.

He explained to Julie that there was a professional matter he had to deal with urgently, and he went in search of a man he knew who liked to be known simply as Quill. Quill was a man of many talents who would do most things for money, for he had a bad gambling habit and was often in debt, a fact that Crichton was able to use to his own advantage.

Quill was a mere five feet two inches tall, thin, light on his feet and quick of movement, with eyes that were forever alert and watchful. Most folk gave him a wide berth, knowing him to be as dangerous as a disturbed rattler. He had undertaken many tasks for Crichton in the past and been well rewarded. So when he found himself in Crichton's office after sundown he was keen to learn how he could be of service.

'I want you to do a little job for me,' Crichton said. 'I don't much care how you do it but it's to be done quickly and the law must not get involved. You up for it?'

Quill had no doubts about that, and his expression showed anticipation at the pleasure and the rewards he expected to get. 'Easy,' he said.

The lawyer went on, 'The job's worth two hundred dollars if you do it swiftly and efficiently. Tonight would be ideal. Hundred now, the rest on completion.' He watched Quill's face and was pleased to see that the mention of so much money had ignited the man's interest like nothing else would.

He paused to let the message sink in and, when Quill nodded, he continued, 'You understand I must not be connected in any way with this . . . er . . . action.'

When Quill nodded again he explained what he wanted, then he reached into a desk drawer and withdrew a bundle of notes. 'Small denominations won't be so obvious,' he said, and handed them across.

'Consider it already done,' Quill said, and pocketed the money without counting it.

Crichton smiled. 'I shall be leaving town for a while. As soon as I know the job's done you'll find the rest of the money in the usual place. And there's something more that may interest you. If you get the chance to look through their pockets you may find a few dollars there.'

'Thanks,' Quill said. 'Is that all you want from me, Mr Randolph?'

'It's enough by my reckoning. Now leave by the back door, but make sure nobody sees you.'

Quill rose and left the office without another word.

Crichton sat for a few minutes, allowing his mind to examine the plans he had made in case he had forgotten anything. Satisfied, he gave a last look around the office. Everything was as it should be. He would not be returning.

Later today he would be married. The following morning he and Julie would be leaving on the stage bound for Elsewhere, a strange name for a town but apt in the circumstances, he thought. He had money there; a very substantial amount that he had deposited in the bank under a false name over a number of years. Now he needed to pick it up.

Once that was done they could travel by train the rest of the journey to the East, where a man and a woman could lose themselves and start a new life. He wondered what Julie's reaction would be when he told her everything, as he intended to do. He smiled when he thought of the town council's reaction when he failed to come back.

★ ★ ★

Quill relished the task he had been given, not just on account of the money but because he hadn't had the satisfaction of shooting anyone lately. He pondered how he was going to achieve it, and it wasn't until after the third glass of whiskey that the idea came to him. It was wild and required an element of luck to make it work. Quill reckoned it was worth trying. If it didn't succeed he would think of some other way.

It was not a good notion to challenge the two men face to face because it would be he, Quill, who would be lying face down in the dirt. He had rejected that option early on. The easy way would be to shoot them in the back after they left the saloon, but it seemed to Quill that they were not about to leave very soon, if at all. Their interest appeared to be taken up with drink, gambling and women. These three activities would probably keep them fully occupied all night, and he couldn't wait.

He left his place at the bar and sauntered over to the table where Cas and Rufus were playing cards with two other men, Bull and Sanchez. Quill knew them well and usually kept clear of them. There was one empty chair.

It seemed that Cas was on a winning streak, and that suited Quill's purpose perfectly. He circled the table, pausing now and again as if he'd lost interest.

'You gonna stand there all day?' Bull growled as he threw his cards on the table. 'Or are ya gonna fill that chair? Then mebbe my luck'll turn.'

Quill accepted the invitation, something he would never do in normal circumstances on account of he preferred to choose his own table. 'Yeah, I'm willin' to take ya money.' He knew that, given average luck, or even without it, he would have no difficulty in winning. He was a skilled player.

But that was not what he intended to do. He sat and smiled to himself when the first cards dealt to him held the basis for a winning hand. Nevertheless he managed to lose that one and the six hands that followed. Bull and Sanchez lost five of them and the dollars were building up in front of Cas and Rufus.

Quill managed to appear disheartened, as did Bull, who was becoming increasingly angry. When the next hand was under way Quill slipped two high cards on to the floor under the table, and then flipped them across with his foot so that they lay under Cas's chair. Then he leaned across and whispered into Bull's ear. The man's face went red and he shoved his chair back, rising with a grunt of fury.

'Stand up,' he snarled, addressing Cas and Rufus. 'Git on ya feet!' His hand hovered over his gun.

The two men stared. 'What the hell fer?' Cas demanded. Nevertheless they stood, sensing danger. Sanchez also rose, his eyes mere slits.

Bull heaved the table aside, spilling cards and money to the floor. 'What're those cards doin' under ya chair?' He pointed to the two aces, lying face up where Cas had been sitting.

Quill considered he'd done enough and started to sidle away, out of the path of the bullets that were likely to be splitting the air. He'd taken only one step when he felt Bull's grip tighten on his arm.

'You stay where ya are,' Bull grated. 'I'm gonna teach these two cheats a lesson. But first they're gonna give us our money back.'

Cas and Rufus showed no signs of wanting to do that. Quite the opposite, for their hands were ominously close to their Colts as the word 'cheat' had been levelled against them.

'They're not our cards.' Rufus kicked one of them across the floor. 'More'n likely they're yours.'

'What would I be doin' with 'em? You're the varmints who've bin winning. Now, yer gonna pick up all those dollars and give them over.'

'I got another idea,' Cas grated. 'You

apologize an' we leave.'

'You ain't goin' nowhere till we settle this.'

'Then draw if ya wanna make ya accusation stick.'

Quill may have been very good with cards but he was no gun-slick. He decided that, in the almost certain event that there would be lead flying, he was going to be the first to draw. His hand reached for his Colt. He yelled a warning to Bull.

'Look out! They're gonna shoot!'

Bull, reacting to the warning, moved fast, his gun appearing in his hand. Cas and Rufus responded swiftly.

Now Quill really wished he could be somewhere else where he could watch the action without being part of it. He had no choice in the matter, as three pistols left their holsters in a blur of movement. He fired a split second before the others and watched Cas and Rufus go down.

Bull had also taken a slug, but he was still on his feet, although his face was white and blood was running down his arm. Sanchez had not fired.

Quill stared down at his own smoking gun, not sure whether he or Bull had fired the fatal shots, for Cas and Rufus were not moving. There was brief silence in the saloon following the roar of the Colts, then voices began to intrude on Quill's thoughts.

'Fetch the marshal!' someone yelled.

Men bent over the prostrate bodies. 'Dead! Both dead.'

Quill sheathed his gun and tried to sneak from the scene, but two men barred his way. 'Wait there, mister. The law's coming.'

'It was self-defence,' Quill said, scooping up some of the money lying loose on the table. 'Ya all saw it.'

The men were having none of it. 'Tell that to the law.'

Quill waited. He was beginning to realize that he had achieved his aim, but at what cost? Sure, it was self-defence like he said. That much was obvious, and he had plenty of witnesses, didn't he?

Marshal Scott McQuade was at the scene within three minutes. His gaze rested on the two bodies on the floor.

'Every one of ya stay exactly where ya are,' he commanded. He bent to examine the men, then turned to the men gathered around.

'Fetch the doc fer that man,' he said, indicating Bull. 'An' the undertaker fer them while yer about it.'

As someone ran off to do his bidding he asked with an edge to his voice, 'What happened here?'

'Seems like them two were cheating,' the barkeep told him. 'Bull an' this feller challenged 'em about it.'

'Who drew first?'

The varying opinions on what had actually occurred did not improve the marshal's patience. He turned his attention to Quill. 'You bin hurt?'

Quill shook his head. 'They was cheating. Bull wanted his money back. Then they decided they wasn't gonna

114

do that an' they pulled their guns.'

'You sayin' they drew first?'

'Yeah. It was self-defence. We didn't have no choice.'

The marshal looked for confirmation. The general opinion was that it probably was self-defence, although some thought otherwise. He reached a decision.

'Party's over,' he declared. 'Get this mess cleaned up an' go about yer business.'

8

Quill began to gather up some more of the spilled money, then, for the third time he attempted to leave.

He was called back by the marshal. 'Not you! Yer comin' down to the office with me. Now!'

Quill shrugged. 'Nothin' much else I kin tell ya,' he said.

'We'll see about that.' McQuade urged him out through the batwings and followed as they made their way to the law office. Once inside he had Quill sit in the chair opposite his desk while he took his time in lighting up a cheroot and pouring out a measure of whiskey into a glass. Quill licked his lips, but was not invited to share.

McQuade leaned back. His chair groaned. 'Three dead bodies and one man wounded in as many hours,' he

began. 'Everythin' seems to be happe-
nin' at once.'

'Three bodies?' Quill asked, inno-
cently. He knew how Charles Hinckley
had died but had not shared that
information with anyone, considering
that it was healthier to stay ignorant.

'Yep. Charles Hinckley was found
down by the livery. Dead. Know
anythin' about that?'

'Why in tarnation should I know
about that?' He had in fact been in the
vicinity of the livery when he had heard
the report of the lawyer's small gun and
had seen Crichton Randolph hurrying
from the scene.

'Just a wild guess,' McQuade said.
'Yer usually found near by when there's
trouble.' He smiled for the first time.
Then he suddenly asked, 'Where'd ya
git the money to gamble?'

The question took Quill by surprise.
'I had it put by from earlier winnings. I
bet I could take some offa you in a
game,' he added, trying for some
humour to lighten the situation.

'That's not likely to happen,' the lawman said. 'Now,' he paused as if he was giving much thought to what he was about to say, 'now, what am I gonna do with you? I've had cause to haul you into this office many times, but ya allus seem to have an explanation fer what you did an' I've had to let you go.'

Quill gazed intently at him. What the hell was he saying: that he believed the death of the two men was his fault? 'I ain't done nothin' wrong,' he growled.

McQuade shook his head. 'I'm not satisfied. I'm gonna lock ya up fer a spell 'til ya tell me what's goin' on. Hand over yer weapon an' stand up.' His own gun was now in his hand, preventing any false moves from Quill, who stood up, reluctantly removed his Colt and laid it on the desk.

'Ya've no cause.'

The marshal slid the gun into a drawer and withdrew a bunch of keys. He jangled them in front of Quill's face. 'Of course, if ya tell me what I wanna know then I'm sure I'd be able to overlook what you've done.'

'I ain't done nothin', Marshal,' Quill repeated. He knew well enough why the marshal was questioning him. He'd been in trouble many times. His acquaintance with both the lawyer and Charles Hinckley was known to McQuade, although Hinckley's death could not possibly be laid at his door.

He reckoned that the less he said the less likely he was to give McQuade reason for holding him. 'Lock me up if yer want to, but I got nothin' to say.'

He stood and walked towards the cell block.

McQuade followed him, pushed him into the cell and closed and locked the door. He turned to go, swung back. 'Naturally,' he said, 'I'm gonna question the men in the saloon some more, an' if I find out it weren't self-defence I reckon you could be facing the rope.'

'I told ya — '

'Yeah, I know. Ya ain't done nothin' wrong. But seeming ya've had yer pockets full o' dollars lately.'

'I've bin lucky at the table,' Quill said.

The marshal, leaning against the bars of the cell, stroked his chin. 'There's more goin' on here than I kin get a handle on. It's all gotta bad smell about it. Until I kin get to the bottom of it yer gonna remain where ya are, so ya'd best git comfortable.'

Quill sucked in his breath. 'But Marshal, I told ya everthin' I know. This ain't fair.'

'Fair or not, Quill, I'm gonna hold ya on suspicion of unlawful killin'.'

Quill came to the conclusion that arguing with the marshal would get him nowhere. 'What about somethin' to fill my belly, then? Ya not aimin' to starve me to death, are ya?'

'All in good time.' McQuade grinned. 'Any time ya feel like talkin' ya kin yell, an' if I'm not busy mebbe I'll come an' hear what ya have to say.' He turned away, then stopped as if he had just thought of something. 'There could be some sorta reward in it fer you if you've got some useful information. The town council's very keen fer me to clear up these killin's an' keep a tidy town.'

Without giving Quill the chance to reply he strode into his office, slamming the door shut behind him.

Quill was in no position to see the satisfied grin on the marshal's face.

★   ★   ★

The wedding of Crichton Randolph, the eminent lawyer, to his beautiful young bride, was a small affair. A few folk turned up to witness the occasion. Quill was not one of them.

After the ceremony Crichton proudly took Julie's arm as they acknowledged the smiles and congratulations of the crowd. For Julie the day had been a mixture of happiness and confusion. A few days ago she had been no more than a woman of little consequence, toiling for her adoptive parents; now she was a married woman, wife of a respected and wealthy lawyer.

Later, when she and her husband were alone, she asked him, 'Why do we have to leave here? You have position and influence. You know so many people and they respect you.'

Crichton answered more sharply than he intended. 'I've already told you, my dear. I have business interests all over the country, connections with important and powerful men in the East. I need to develop them.' He was thoughtful for a moment. 'There's a lot you don't know about me, Julie. I'm ambitious, still young enough to climb the ladder of success. I've done all I can in this backwater. What I have here is not important, merely a stepping stone to better things.

'And,' he added in a softer tone, 'with you beside me there is no limit to what I can achieve. Life's gonna be good for us, Julie. We'll have everything we could possibly want. My ma and pa didn't make it, but I intend to. They worked hard but were swindled out of their land and their money. That's not gonna happen to us.'

Julie looked at him, seeing in him a hardness she had not noticed before, but respecting him for what he was trying to do. 'I understand,' she said. 'You have my support.'

He seemed pleased to accept this assurance. 'We'll be travelling first thing tomorrow. The stage leaves just after sunup. Best get an early night.'

Later they ate well and retired to their room in the hotel. Crichton made a surprisingly considerate lover. They were awakened early as arranged and ate a good breakfast of porridge, followed by eggs and corn fritters. This was the biggest breakfast Julie had ever had and she enjoyed it.

'There's a long and tiring day ahead of us,' Crichton told her. 'When we get to Elsewhere we can rest before we continue our journey by train.'

The stage pulled out on time and they both settled back in their seats, knowing that the sun would make its entire trip across the sky before they reached their destination.

There were three other passengers travelling with them from Redstone Creek that day: an older gentleman who gave them a smile with tired eyes, and a younger couple who only had eyes for each other. Other folk came and went at the various stops. Few seemed to be in the mood for talking, and Julie was content to rest her head on Crichton's shoulder and catch up on some sleep.

★　★　★

It was McQuade's intention that Quill should spend an uncomfortable night. Having shut the cell door, he had no intention of opening it again for a good spell. He figured that a period of isolation might serve to soften up his reluctant prisoner who, the marshal reckoned, knew much more than he was telling; not just about the killings, but also of his business dealings with

Crichton Randolph.

Of course, he'd have to feed him sometime, but he'd got water and was in no danger of starving. Maybe later he would crack the intervening door open and let the aroma of coffee and beef stew drift into the cells.

But the marshal was disappointed if he expected a quick reaction from Quill, and he felt it necessary the following morning to take some food in to him. Not beef stew or coffee, naturally. Bread and a hunk of cheese would fill his belly and give him a hankering for more.

'How's yer investigation goin', Marshal?' Quill asked when he'd stuffed some of the food into his mouth.

McQuade eyed him quizzically. 'D'ya really wanna know?'

'Wouldn't've asked otherwise.'

'Well as I coulda hoped,' McQuade said.

'That don't say much. An' it don't say much fer this grub. What about some beef an' gravy from Anna's

125

Kitchen? She does great food.'

The marshal smiled broadly. 'Reckon you'll be here fer a spell yet, so ya'd best git used to what the town can afford.'

'Ya cain't hold me,' Quill growled.

'Only 'til they git the rope to hang ya.'

The lawman studied his prisoner. Was it his imagination or did he see a hint of anxiety and doubt in Quill's eyes? He let his gaze rest on the other man until Quill was forced to look away. Without a word he turned and walked away, but had only reached the door to his office when Quill called him back.

Quill clutched the bars of his cell. 'I got sometin' to tell ya,' he said, the words coming out rapidly in his eagerness to be heard.

'Glad to hear it,' McQuade said. 'Mebbe we'd best go into my office. If yer story's good an' if I believe it, I've got some liquor we could try.' He produced the keys and unlocked the cell door. 'No tricks, now, or sure as hell I'll hang the charge of unlawful killin' on ya head.'

They settled themselves on either side of the desk. 'I'm listenin'. You do the talkin',' McQuade said.

Quill pointed to the bottle. 'Sure, but what about a taste o' that whiskey afore I start? My tongue feels like it's covered in sand.'

McQuade hesitated, then relented and poured them both a good measure. Quill downed his in one swallow and pushed his glass across for more.

'I ain't heard nothin' yet,' the marshal said.

Quill drew a deep breath. 'It's like this. Now an' agin I do a few little jobs fer Crichton Randolph,' he began. 'He pays well.'

The marshal felt a tinge of excitement as Quill's words seemed to confirm the doubts that he'd held about the lawyer. 'Go on.'

'Fact is,' Quill continued, 'I still got cash to pick up fer my last job, but you hauled me off before I could get it. I'll show ya if ya want, but it's my money.'

McQuade nodded. 'Later. What was the payment fer?'

Quill was silent for so long that the marshal wondered if he had had second thoughts. 'I'm waitin'.'

'Fer makin' sure Cas an' Rufus couldn't talk no more.'

'You killed them!'

Quill shot out of his seat. 'No! That's not how it was. I'm only tellin' ya what I was paid to do. But I didn't do it! I made sure my shots went wide.'

Once started, Quill couldn't stop and, plied with another glass of liquor, he continued to talk for the next ten minutes.

At the end of that time the marshal said, 'I'm gonna release ya, but yer to stay in town. That understood? If ya try to leave I'll hunt ya down an' kill ya.'

He watched as Quill left his office. Then he hurried down to the telegraph office.

9

It had all gone wrong. In the first raid carried out by the Coyote Gang two people had been killed. Murder had not been Saul's intention, but it had occurred and there was nothing that could be done about that. He cursed Seth for being so quick with his weapon.

'We'd best lie low fer a while,' he said as they pulled up at the edge of town. 'Act normal as if nothin's happened.'

'What about my arm?' Brett whined. 'There's a slug in there. It's gotta come out, an' I'm bleedin' somethin' bad.'

'Can't go to the doc, not after what we've done,' Saul said. 'We've gotta take it out ourselves.'

'Ya can't do that!' Brett screamed.

'It'll be easy,' Saul assured him. 'I seen how my pa took a slug outa a steer when it got shot accidental. There's nothin' to it. Least you'll have a good slug o' whiskey beforehand, which the cow didn't have the pleasure of.' He grinned broadly. 'It'll teach ya not to be so easy with yer gun.'

Brett scowled. 'I'm goin' to the doc.'

'No you ain't.'

'Ya ain't touchin' me. Neither of ya. I ain't no goddamn steer. Was your fault I got shot.'

Saul laughed. 'Dunno how ya make that out. I seen children with more backbone than you. It'd be easy enough with a good dose of liquor. Depends how deep the slug is.' He took a step towards Brett. 'Let's have a look.'

Brett jumped back as if he'd been branded. 'No! I told ya, I'm goin' to the doc.'

'We could all get strung up for this mornin's work.'

'The doc's old. We could threaten him so's he wouldn't talk.'

Saul considered this. 'Mebbe. Considerin' ya so scared o' a little pain. I don't like it but it's probably fer the

130

best. We'll make fer Doc O'Halloran's place. Mebbe get there before there's many folk about.' He gazed at Brett's pale face. 'Yer'll have to look natural if anybody sees ya. Can ya do that?'

Brett nodded, relieved that he would not have to face the amateur surgery that Saul had suggested, which would probably have left him in a worse state than he already was.

They entered town separately. Although it was still early there were some folk beginning to appear. Saul was first to arrive at the doc's door. It was of solid, polished wood with a brass plate attached, engraved with the doc's name, followed by MD. Saul knocked, waited briefly and knocked again, harder this time. He heard footsteps within the house, then the door opened.

Doc O'Halloran stared at him with bleary eyes. He was about sixty years old, a slight figure with stooped shoulders and wispy grey hair. He was still attired in his nightshirt and was fiddling with his spectacles as he attempted to fit them on to his eyes.

'Yes?' he asked.

'My friend's bin hurt,' Saul said.

The doc let his gaze wander to left and right. 'Where is he?'

'He'll be along in a minute or so.'

'What's wrong with him?'

Saul hesitated. 'You'll see when he gets here. Can I wait inside?'

The doc reluctantly stepped aside and beckoned Saul in. 'Better be important. Haven't eaten yet.'

The door opened on to a large vestibule, floored with polished tiles. Beyond that, the house stretched back, providing space much larger than appeared from the outside. Several doors opened from the hallway and a flight of carpeted stairs led to an upper floor.

Before the door closed they heard the clatter of hoofs. Brett reined in and slid from the saddle. His face had gone deathly white and he found difficulty standing. Saul quickly took his elbow and pulled him into the house.

The medic took one look and led the way into rear room that served as his surgery. After a brief examination he turned to Saul. 'He's taken a bullet,' he said. 'I reckon the sheriff should be told about this. Go fetch him.'

Saul didn't move. 'No cause to get the law. Just get the slug out an' ferget you ever saw us.'

Doc O'Halloran's eyes showed suspicion. 'We'll see about that soon as I've put some clothes on. Meanwhile, don't just stand there. Help me get him up on to that table and remove his clothing. He seems to've lost a lot of blood.'

Still in his nightshirt the doc plugged the wound in Brett's shoulder. 'I'm gonna get dressed,' he told Saul. 'Make sure he doesn't fall off.'

By the time the doc had dressed himself and returned to the surgery his patient was moaning and only half conscious. Saul was waiting impatiently, though his face showed little sympathy for Brett's discomfort.

'Ya took ya time,' he said.

The doc testily adjusted the glasses on the bridge of his nose. 'Go wait outside. There's nothing more you can do here.'

There was a loud hammering on the front door and the doc looked up in annoyance. 'See who that is. I'm expecting a call from a lady about to give birth.'

But when Saul opened the door he was met with Seth, red-faced and flustered. 'Bumped into the goddamn deputy sheriff,' Seth blurted out. 'Asked me what I was doin' up so early.'

Saul dragged him inside. 'What the hell did ya tell him?'

'Told him it were none of his business.'

'An' he let ya go?'

'Yeah, 'course he did. Nothin' to hold me on.'

Saul remained thoughtful. 'News'll be quick in comin',' he said. 'Miles Pitcher ain't no Chas Morgan an' he won't be long in putting two and two together. We gotta be careful. Best thing you kin do is make out you were visiting some gal somewhere. Have ya got someone in mind who'll back up ya story?'

'Yep. Got more'n one.' Seth grinned.

Saul shoved him towards the door. 'One'll do. Git moving now.'

'What about the doc? How're ya gonna keep him quiet?'

Saul slapped his gun. 'Leave the doc to me. He ain't gonna be openin' his mouth.'

Seth left and Saul waited until Doc O'Halloran appeared from the surgery. 'Your friend will be fine,' the doc said. 'How'd he come by being shot?'

Saul took his arm, propelled him to the nearest chair, and stood looking down at him. 'Best thing you kin do, Doc, is not to ask no questions an' to keep ya mouth shut. This ain't somethin' that anybody else needs to know about.'

When the doc opened his mouth in protest Saul slid a knife from his belt and continued as if speaking to a naughty child. 'I know ya feel as how ya wanna tell someone, but I'll just remind you how pretty ya daughter is, an' it would be a shame if she suffered any harm just on account of you gabbin' about what's happened here.'

This time the doc said nothing and the silence lengthened.

'Your friend'll have to stay here for a day or so,' the doc said at last, the expression on his face a mixture of fear and anger.

'Well, that'll be jest fine, then.' Saul sheathed the knife. He turned and left Doc O'Halloran still seated and breathing heavily.

★   ★   ★

Kate had risen early and was up and breakfasted before the sun had showed itself. She had told her friend what she was hoping to do, and both of them agreed that it was not going to be easy. Folk were not ready to come forward to say what they'd seen, even though it might mean that a man would be falsely accused of murder.

She was convinced that Brad was innocent and she was determined to find someone who had witnessed the killing and was willing to speak out.

'It's their duty!' she told Marylou. But she wasn't sure that anyone would see it that way.

Her first visit was to the Silver Spur saloon, where she hoped to speak to the barkeep. She was disappointed, therefore, when she found that the man behind the bar had not been on duty the day before.

She took a moment to study the interior. This was her very first experience of being in the saloon and she wondered why men seemed to like it so much. The odours of tobacco and drink still hung in the air from the night before and stung her nostrils. There were no customers at this time of the morning. The barkeep looked down at her from where he was polishing the large mirror that hung behind the bar. He was a young man, lean and wiry with a mop of brown hair.

'What kin I do fer you, young lady? I reckon yer not here fer the liquor.'

She walked up to the polished counter. 'Do you know what went on here last night?'

'Nope. Didn't see it. I only come in mornings to clear up the mess.'

She showed her disappointment. 'Then you don't know what happened when a man got shot?'

He shook his head. 'I heard about it from Old Sol who runs the barbershop down the street. But he won't be there jus' yet.'

He must have seen Kate's face fall because he continued, 'At this time of day you'll find him at home if it's important to you. No more'n a wood shack at the end of East, offa Main. Tell him I sent ya, an' if he tells ya what ya want to know I'll set up a glass fer him.'

Kate thanked him and left, glad to be away from the unfamiliar smells. She had just set off along the main drag when she noticed, some fifty yards away, three horses standing outside the surgery of Doc O'Halloran.

Something about the animals was familiar, and as she approached she realized what that was. She recognized them and guessed that Saul and his worthless cronies must be near by, probably in the doc's. For what purpose she could only imagine, but she intended to find out.

She had just reached the decision to knock on the doc's door when her attention was distracted by a flurry of activity outside the law office. A rider had reined in sharply, slid from his horse and was pounding on the sheriff's door. Several folk had stopped what they were doing to see what the noise was about.

Kate shrugged. She had to finish one thing at a time, and she continued on her way to look for Old Sol. One willing witness might encourage others to come forward, providing a weight of evidence the sheriff could not ignore.

Old Sol's cabin surprised her. Small though it was, it was well cared for with fresh white paint decorating the walls, and flowers lining the path that led to the front door.

Kate knocked and the door was opened almost immediately by a man of about fifty, smartly dressed in grey pants and white shirt. His hair was already thinning. He smiled and invited her in before she had uttered a word.

They sat in the small front room on two wooden chairs. 'Saw you coming,' he said. 'I know you. Seen you around. You're Kate, ain't you? I've seen you with that new brother of yourn, Brad, when he's come in to get his hair cut.'

His voice was gentle and friendly and Kate responded, immediately at ease.

'That's why I've come to see you,' she said, diving straight in. 'Brad's in jail. The sheriff locked him up for something he didn't do. I know he didn't because he couldn't kill anyone. Not 'less he was forced to.'

Sol held up his hand before she could go on. 'I've bin thinkin' about that. You must understand, young lady, that folk around here have learned to keep silent. Your real brother, Saul, is bad, a waster, if you'll forgive me for speaking bluntly. He's apt to react violently if folk cross him. His sidekicks are the same, though they've only one brain between them.'

'But — ' Kate began, but again Sol stopped her.

'You're here to ask me to tell the law what I seen, ain't ya? An' I'm glad, on account of I've bin ashamed I didn't speak up at the time. Yep, I saw what happened. It was self-defence fer sure. Fact is, I don't believe yer brother meant to pull the trigger at all. Probably accidental, and I'm prepared to tell Miles Pitcher that right now.'

They rose together and went out into the morning sun. They walked quickly towards the law office, where they could see several horses at the hitch rail.

'Somethin's up,' Sol observed as they drew closer.

They knocked and pushed the door open to find Miles Pitcher, his deputy Chas Morgan and three other men crowded into the small office. The sheriff looked up as they entered, his eyes flicking from Kate to Sol and back again.

'I'm a mite busy jus' now,' he said, brusquely.

'It's important.' Kate almost shouted in her frustration.

'So's this,' Miles Pitcher told her. 'Come back later an' my deputy'll deal with it.'

'Brad's innocent,' Kate blurted out. 'You've got to let him go. Sol saw it all.'

The sheriff didn't bother to hide his annoyance. 'That so, Sol?'

Sol nodded. 'Self-defence. No doubt about it.'

'An' ya didn't bother to tell me this afore now?' Pitcher inclined his head. 'I'll see to it when I git back. There's bin two killings out at this man's farm. We're setting out there right now.'

For the first time Kate noticed the distraught look on the face of one of the men. 'Oh,' she breathed, feeling guilty at being so full of her own problem. Then her eyes blazed. 'You've got an innocent man locked up, Sheriff.'

The sheriff's face turned red with anger. 'I told ya, I'm dealin' with two cold-blooded murders. I ain't about to release a prisoner just 'cause you come bustin' in with a story 'bout a witness. The jail will still be here when I come back. Then I'll consider what yer tellin' me. Not before.'

Kate stood her ground. 'You've locked up an innocent man, Miles Pitcher, and I'm not moving out of your office until you let him go.'

The sheriff was taken aback. His silver star meant that folk did as he told them. He looked from one person to the other.

'I'll vouch fer him,' Sol said.

'All you have to do is turn the key and let him go,' Kate pleaded.

The lawman shrugged as if he found

it difficult to understand women.

'He means somethin' to ya, huh?' He turned to Sol. 'I'm releasing him on your say-so, Sol.' Then to his deputy he said, 'See to it, Chas.' With that he strode out of the door, followed swiftly by the other men, leaving Kate and Sol in the glowering presence of Chas Morgan.

The deputy leered at Kate. 'Well, well. Couldn't keep away from me, could ya?'

'Just do like the sheriff told you,' Sol said. 'The sooner we get outa here the better.'

Chas Morgan moved slowly. As he unhooked the keys and went into the cell block he muttered, 'Don't reckon it's right. Not right at all.'

They heard the rattle of the keys in the lock, then Morgan came through the intervening door still muttering to himself, followed by Brad, who was smiling broadly.

'Just getting comfortable,' he joked. He nodded to Sol and then fixed his

144

gaze on Kate. 'I'm obliged to both of you.'

He took Kate in his arms and embraced her. He held on for a long moment with the sudden knowledge that he had never done that before now. It was a pleasant feeling.

'Git out afore I'm sick to the stomach,' Chas growled. They left willingly.

'Where're ya going now?' Brad asked. He shook Sol's hand.

Sol smiled. 'I gotta business to run. An' you need a haircut. Pop in when yer've got the time. This one's free.'

Brad looked questioningly at Kate. 'I've got supplies an' hosses to take back home.'

'They're at the livery,' she told him.

'Will you be coming home with me?'

Kate gave it some thought. 'Later,' she said. 'There's something else I have to find out.' She had achieved what she had set out to do, but now another matter was claiming her attention. The fact that her brother had spent some time at Doc O'Halloran's intrigued her. She had to find out why.

She kissed Sol on the cheek. 'Thanks, Sol. I owe you.'

'We both do,' Brad agreed.

Kate put her hand on Brad's arm and felt her heart beat faster when he laid his hand briefly on top of hers. 'Tell Pa I'll be back soon.'

She watched both men as they went on their way. She had never allowed herself to think of Brad as anything but a brother. The realization that he had become something else entirely came as rather a shock, and surprised her by its intensity.

She made her way thoughtfully to Doc O'Halloran's surgery.

10

After Saul had left Doc O'Halloran's Seth was happy to rest. He had enjoyed his exhausting visit to a certain young lady who had promised to uphold his story that he had been with her all night. Seth had been quite persuasive on that point and the girl had been quick to agree, not relishing the sensation of the edge of Seth's knife on her face.

'How's my pard?' he asked.

The doc waved his hand. 'Go see him if you want. He'll be ready to leave before long.'

'How soon will that be?'

'Not soon enough!'

Seth opened the door to the surgery and peered round. 'He's still sleeping like a baby. Sure you ain't killed him?'

'I don't kill folk.'

Seth closed the door. 'Got any liquor

in the house, Doc?' he asked.

The doc produced a bottle which he reluctantly handed over, knowing that Seth would search for it anyway. 'You've got what you want. Now I need to do my rounds.'

Seth took a long drink from the bottle and rose to his feet. 'You ain't goin' nowhere,' he grated.

The doc sighed wearily. 'If I don't folk'll come looking for me. Then there'll be some explainin' to do. What's it gonna be?'

Seth wasn't equipped to make decisions like this. 'If I let ya go jus' remember what'll happen to ya if ya say anythin' about this. 'Sfar as you're concerned it never happened.'

Doc O'Halloran gathered up his medical bags. 'Saul made himself very clear on that point.' He cast an angry look at Seth and made his way to the front door. Just before he reached it someone knocked hard on the outside.

'Git rid of 'em,' Seth ordered.

But whoever it was wasn't taking no

148

for an answer, and Seth was surprised as Kate pushed her way into the room. The doc followed her.

'What's going on?' Kate asked. 'Saul was here earlier, wasn't he? Now I find you here and I'll wager Brett's not far away.'

Seth's eyes strayed towards the surgery door. Kate followed his gaze and looked questioningly at the doc.

'My guess would be that the third worthless member of your band's been wounded. You been treating him, Doc?'

'What's that to you?' Seth snarled.

Doc O'Halloran nodded. 'Yes, I had to patch up a bullet wound.'

'Is he bad?'

'He'll live,' the doc said. 'Had to dig the slug out. No serious injury, but he'll need to recover from the surgery.'

Kate turned to Seth. 'How'd it happen?'

Seth showed his teeth. 'None o' yer business.'

'Where's Saul now?'

'Dunno.' Seth took another mouthful

from the bottle he was holding.

Kate was thoughtful for a moment. Then she turned to the doc. 'A farmer and his wife have been killed. Shot down outside their home early this morning. I think maybe the sheriff'll be interested in anyone coming in with a bullet in them.'

'I agree,' the doc said. He appeared to be embarrassed. 'I, er, haven't been able to leave here, otherwise I'd've told him myself.'

Kate appeared to understand. 'Miles Pitcher is out there at the farm with a posse just now. I suppose I'll have to report it to Chas Morgan.'

Seth took a hurried step forward. His mind had been working on the problem, which was growing too big for him to handle but he had reached a decision of sorts. 'You ain't leavin', neither of ya.'

Kate didn't flinch. 'You aiming to stop me?' She strode purposefully towards the door. 'I'm leaving right now.'

Seth hadn't thought that far. He quickly grabbed her arm. He was certainly strong enough to hold her, to stop her. Fact was he had a gun at his hip and he could cover Kate and the doc with that. But what then? If the sheriff got to know of Brett's injury the game would be up.

Kate shook herself free. 'Let me go! You can't keep a thing like this quiet.'

'Saul wants to talk to ya,' Seth said quickly. 'Afore ya do anything,' he added.

Kate showed surprise. 'My brother hasn't spoken to me for long enough. Where is he?'

Seth relaxed a little. Perhaps he was handling the situation better than he feared. 'I'll take ya to him.'

'You told me you didn't know where he was,' Kate said.

'Yeah, well, I do, an' he said as how I was to take ya to him.' He saw doubt in Kate's eyes. 'That is, if I was to see you. An' now here ya are.' He glared at the doc, challenging him to say anything.

'You stay here an' take care of yer patient. Ya know what ya have to do. And,' he added with a sneer, 'what not to do.'

He led Kate through the passageway and out of the back door of the house. 'Gotta go out this way. When ya've talked to Saul ya kin make up yer mind what ya wanna do.'

He felt Kate's reluctance but it didn't matter now, even when she swung round.

'This isn't right,' she began, but that was as far as she got. Seth's gun swept up and round viciously to connect with her temple. She groaned and sank to the ground.

Seth hauled her up and draped her over his shoulder. She was moaning but had not recovered sufficiently to call out. The problem now was to avoid being seen. The sun was not yet high enough to penetrate the back lots, but there was enough light for anyone to recognize him.

He felt panic rise in his throat. He

turned left and ran, his burden bumping against his shoulder but hardly slowing him down. There was only one place he could take her where he believed she could be safely secured. He would have to tie her up. If he bound her securely enough and gagged her he could tell Saul and he would know what to do.

Where the hell *was* Saul?

★　★　★

Chas Morgan liked power, the authority given him by his position as deputy sheriff of a busy town like Elsewhere. While Miles Pitcher was away dealing with the murders at the homestead, he sat comfortably in the big leather chair, put his feet up on the desk, fired up a stogie and re-read the telegram that had arrived that morning.

FROM SCOTT MCQUADE, MARSHAL OF REDSTONE CREEK TO MILES PITCHER, SHERIFF OF ELSEWHERE.

STAGECOACH DUE YOUR TOWN TODAY. EXPECT MAN AND WIFE, NEWLY MARRIED. MAN ABOUT THIRTY, WOMAN YOUNGER. MAN, CRICHTON RANDOLPH, DANGER-OUS. SUSPECTED OF KILLING. PROBABLY CARRYING LARGE SUM OF STOLEN MONEY. BELIEVE WOMAN TO BE INNOCENT. SUG-GEST YOU DETAIN HIM UNTIL I ARRIVE WITH THE EVIDENCE. APPRECIATE YOUR COOPERATION.

Chas Morgan checked his gun. There was time yet to finish his cigar. Then, perhaps he could take a walk about the town, swagger a little, until he made the arrest. The thought caused him to draw heavily on his cigar, and a thick curl of blue smoke swirled above his head.

At length he rose and strolled out into the midday sun, relishing the thought of the arrest he was about to make. Most of the cells had been empty for several days and this fact didn't sit easily with the deputy, who considered that folk only respected the law when it showed its teeth.

★ ★ ★

Saul watched the stagecoach pull up outside the hotel. It had become a habit for him to assess the passengers as they alighted. Most were of no interest to him, but sometimes he recognized likely prey, someone he could rob. And today his eyes rested on a man and the young girl who accompanied him, who was either his wife or his daughter.

Of even more interest was the presence of Chas Morgan, the deputy sheriff, who strode up to the couple and, with his hand resting on his Colt, addressed the man in aggressive tones. Saul edged nearer.

'Yer name Crichton Randolph?' the deputy asked.

The man was clearly used to being in charge, and showed no signs of backing down in face of such an unwelcoming approach. 'What of it?'

The deputy modified his tone but repeated the question. 'I've had a telegram,' he added by way of explanation.

Crichton stared him down. 'Well, that is exciting. Yep, that's my name. But we're tired, we're covered in dust, we're hungry, an' we just wanna get to our room an' clean up. Can this wait 'til later?'

Chas Morgan's chest swelled and his shoulders went back. In the absence of the sheriff there was nothing he liked better than arresting folk, especially if they resisted.

'Ya comin' with me now. I've bin instructed.'

'Instructed?' Crichton asked.

'Is what I said.'

The lawyer squared up to him. 'Well, I'm instructing you otherwise. I have influence in this territory. I've got powerful friends an' I've got sizeable assets in your bank. I'd expect the law round here to give protection to its citizens, not to harass them fer no reason.'

'I'm the law here. An' I'm arrestin' ya like I've bin told to do.'

'I trust you realize what a serious offence unlawful arrest is,' Crichton said. 'You could end up spending time in prison yerself. I'm a lawyer. I count judges as my friends.'

Saul, watching without appearing to do so, noticed how the deputy took half a step back. His brain, slowed down on account of the whiskey he had so obviously been consuming, was attempting to deal with a situation he hadn't encountered before. The lawyer was educated, professional, knowledge-able in the law, and didn't have the appearance of a criminal.

Chas backed off a little, modifying his tone. 'Only doin' my job,' he said. 'I need to talk to you down at the office. I was hopin' ya'd come willingly.' His hand still kept close to his holster but he stopped short of drawing his weapon.

'Don't mind talking,' Crichton said. 'Yeah, I'll come with you. Jawing never hurt anybody yet. Give me a moment to speak to my wife.'

Saul strained to hear as Crichton took his wife a short distance away. It was obvious, although the two were out of earshot, that the man was giving a lot of attention to the cases that had been off-loaded from the coach and now lay on the sidewalk.

The lawyer pointed to the hotel and his wife nodded, although she looked less than happy.

The spark of interest that had been kindling in Saul's breast glowed brightly. What might be hidden in that luggage?

Chas Morgan was showing signs of impatience. 'C'mon. Ain't got all day.'

Crichton swung round. 'Yeah. Long as it's clean I ain't under arrest.'

The deputy nodded without enthusiasm.

As Crichton left his wife to go with the deputy Saul stepped forward.

'Allow me to help you, ma'am,' he said politely with what he hoped was a friendly smile. 'My name's Saul. I guess you've booked into this here hotel an' ya've got a pile of luggage. I'm at your service.'

He thought he might have overdone it as he felt Crichton's eyes on him, assessing him. Although he was pleased to receive a nod of acceptance from the lawyer, the glance that Chas Morgan favoured him with spoke otherwise.

'Thank you,' Julie said. 'My husband appears to have business to attend to.'

Saul hoisted up two of the heaviest cases. 'Stayin' long?'

'One night, I believe,' she said with a sweet smile. She lifted the remaining two lighter bags.

He sensed that she didn't trust him fully, but he didn't let that worry him. Although she couldn't know it, his reputation around the town was less than good. He led the way into the hotel and rang the bell at the counter. He placed the cases at her feet.

'Thank you,' she said again.

Saul's heart sang. She sure was pretty, just the way he liked them. The situation held promise. Worth waiting for.

The owner of the hotel, a buxom lady of about fifty with powdered hair and a cheery smile, came bustling through from the back room. She cast a baleful glare on Saul, who returned the glare and stayed only long enough to learn the number of Julie's room.

Julie thanked him as he left and he felt a glow of excitement at the thought that, although she was unaware of it, he would be visiting her very soon. After the disastrous raid on the homestead that morning, with two people killed and one of his gang wounded, his need for money was still dominant in his mind. But the woman was pretty, no doubt of that, and had awoken desires within him that needed to be satisfied.

He made for his favourite table in his favourite saloon and sat there nursing a drink of cold beer while he ran through in his mind all that had happened that day. As far as he knew there was nothing to tie him into the raid and the killings except Doc O'Halloran. He wondered if he had put a big enough scare into the man to stop him talking. Perhaps he should do something about that sooner rather than later, before the doc's conscience overcame his fear of Saul's threat.

He finished his drink and walked swiftly to the doc's house and surgery. The front door was locked and he pounded on it. If the doc was there he was playing possum. But, hell, where was Seth? He knocked again with the same result, then realized he was attracting attention from folk passing by. He turned and strolled away as if there was nothing wrong.

He went down the alley and tried the rear door to the surgery. It was locked. Knocking brought no response. God-damn it! Where was Seth? His horse was missing, which meant that he had ridden off somewhere. Dammit! Did the man have no sense? They were supposed to stick together. He began to wonder if Seth could keep his mouth shut.

As he set his feet back up the main drag he was relieved to see Seth coming towards him. Saul pointed to the hotel and Seth reined in there and waited.

Saul showed his anger. 'You left Brett with the doc?'

'Yeah, but — '

'How'd he seem?'

'Scared. Dunno what you said to him, but he weren't goin' nowhere.'

'I expected you to stay with him.'

'Yeah, but I had to — '

'I don't want none of yer excuses. We're s'posed to be a team. Now you're here wait outside. I gotta little job I need to do. When I come out I'll wanna know where ya've been.'

Seth shrugged, seated himself on one of the chairs on the porch, sat back and closed his eyes.

Saul reckoned the young lady would now either be having a bath or have gone for a meal. Either way suited him well. He visualized her naked and vulnerable and his heart pounded. He slipped into the hotel unnoticed and went up the stairs two at a time. The rooms were numbered and he knocked lightly on the door with a number three nailed on it.

Without waiting for an answer he tried the handle but found it locked. He knocked again, harder this time, and was rewarded by sounds within the room. When the key turned in the lock he put his shoulder against the door and shoved hard. As he thrust his way into the room Julie was thrown back.

He closed the door and put his fingers to his lips for silence, reinforcing the sign by drawing his knife.

'I don't wanna hurt ya,' he said. 'I've jus' come to welcome ya to Elsewhere, friendly like.'

Julie said nothing but her eyes blazed as she recovered her balance. Saul was surprised to see anger there rather than fear. He advanced upon her but, instead of backing away, she picked up the large water jug on the washstand and held it aloft.

Saul stretched his lips in a grin. 'Jus' as I like 'em,' he said. He caught hold of the jug, wrested it from her and threw it aside. The knife in his other hand was close to her cheek.

'What's ya name? Julie, ain't it?'

'Get out!' Julie hissed. 'My husband will be here soon.'

'I figure he might be a whiles yet,' Saul said. 'Prob'ly looking at the inside of a cell by now.' His eyes bored into hers. He swung her round and threw her on to the bed where travel bags were partly unpacked. Still keeping his gaze on Julie he began to pull the contents of the bags out and scatter them on the floor. 'Lotta luggage here fer two people.'

He held up some of Julie's clothes. 'Very purty.' Then his searching fingers felt something hard, a large parcel wrapped in cloth and securely tied. He stepped back. 'What's in there? Take it out,' he said, 'an' let's see what's in it.'

Julie lifted the package and laid it on the bed. Saul slashed the bindings with his knife and watched with awe as the wrappings came off. His eyes opened wide as packets of large-denomination bills tumbled out.

'What the . . . ' he exclaimed as he saw that there was yet another parcel in the bottom of the bag. He glanced up as he heard Julie gasp and saw that surprise was etched all over her face. 'Ya didn't know?' He ran his fingers over the money. How much was there? Ten thousand? Twenty thousand? Fifty thousand? A *hundred* thousand? He'd never seen so much money in one place in all his life.

His visit was proving more rewarding than he had anticipated.

'Yes, I knew,' Julie stammered. 'Of course I knew. It's our money. Leave it.'

Saul's mind worked. 'More like it belongs to someone else,' he said. 'Where in tarnation did ya get that? A bank, mebbe? Your husband been robbin' a bank? That why the sheriff's locked him up? You two runnin' away from the law? Well, I reckon this changes things.'

He sheathed his knife so that he could riffle through the bundles, see if they were real. His attention was so concentrated on the money that he did not see Julie as she hurled herself on him, her fingers scratching, her fists pounding.

Saul threw her off but not before she had inflicted some damage to his face. 'You bitch!' he yelled. In a reflex action his hand snaked to his Colt. He withdrew it, cocked it to give emphasis to his words, and pointed it at her. 'Git over there and shuddup,' he grated. 'A man woulda died if he'd done that. I won't hesitate to kill ya if ya try that agin.'

If he expected her to be submissive, facing a loaded gun, he was mistaken.

'Get out of my room,' she screamed, and launched herself at him again. She was like a wildcat. She had fought many battles alongside her brother in the unforgiving city streets; now she brought all that experience to bear.

In the face of the furious attack Saul's gun went off, the bullet bringing down pieces from the ceiling.

Julie's hand flew to her head where blood was already staining her hair, and she sank, first to her knees, then slid to the floor and lay still. Saul stood as he surveyed the damage and the prostrate figure of the girl. 'Dammit to hell!' he cursed.

But there was still the money for the taking. He sheathed his gun, went over to the bed, emptied one of the bags and filled it with the bundles of dollars. 'Worth the effort,' he said triumphantly.

As he hoisted the bag he heard shouts and running footsteps on the stairs and along the corridor. He took out the Colt once more, wrenched open the door and stepped outside the room.

He made for the stairs but was met by Miles Pitcher pounding towards him, six-gun out. Saul didn't hesitate.

He fired and the lawman spun sideways and fell, clutching his right hip.

Saul was now confronted by a second man coming up behind the sheriff whom he recognized as the husband of the woman he had just shot and robbed. Saul didn't wait to see whether the man was armed. He fired for a second time. Crichton took the slug in his chest, where it entered his heart and killed him instantly.

Saul kept running, swerving past the body of the sheriff and leaping over the lawyer, with his Colt ready in his hand to dispense death to anyone foolish or brave enough to get in his way.

He raced down the stairs, bag in one hand, gun in the other, and out through the door into the street. The few folk who had gathered there stepped aside. He'd hardly had time to think, so he was relieved to see Seth waiting with their two mounts saddled and ready. He leaped into the saddle, hooked the bag over the cantle and spurred his horse into action, not caring whether Seth followed.

A shot followed but went nowhere near him. Ahead of him he saw Chas Morgan leap into his path, drawing his gun and bringing it up ready for a shot. The cry of 'Stop' died on the deputy's lips as Saul tried to ride him down.

Then he was clear and away. He didn't even bother to look round to see if Seth was there. If the bullet had found him that wouldn't have worried Saul one bit.

11

Brad and his adoptive parents had been anxiously waiting for Kate's return for most of the day. Brad had been busy but, as the sun went down and there was no sign of his sister, he had made up his mind to go and look for her.

'Did she say where she was going after she got you out of jail?' Sam Finnan asked.

Brad chewed on his lip. 'Said she had somethin' to do. Somethin' to do with Doc O'Halloran. I'm goin' into town. See if I kin find her. It'll be dark soon.'

'She was gonna stay with her friend, Marylou, last night. Best try there first,' Sam said, as Brad saddled his horse, buckled on his gunbelt and set off.

It had been an instinctive reaction to wear his gun. He had a feeling that Kate might have run into trouble and, if

170

that turned out to be the case, he wanted to be ready to deal with it. He urged his horse on, his mind going over all the possible explanations for Kate's absence.

The main thing that troubled him was the thought that Saul might somehow be behind it. Saul was the cause of much that had upset his new parents recently. He knew that they blamed themselves for his wild ways, even though Brad and Kate had tried to persuade them otherwise.

As he rode down the main street of Elsewhere he noticed Seth walking in the direction of the livery. Where that wastrel was, Saul would not be far behind. He was tempted to follow, but decided that his first call had to be on Marylou.

All he learned there was that Kate had left that morning early and had not returned. He received similar results from questioning other folk, some of whom had seen her but not after about midday. As he passed the window of the barber's shop he saw Old Sol closing up for the day.

The old man took the quirley from his mouth. 'Ya gonna let me cut ya hair?' he called, but the laughter died on his lips when he saw the grim expression on Brad's face. 'Trouble?' he asked.

'Ya ain't seen Kate, have ya?' Brad asked without much hope. He was beginning to believe she had been spirited away.

Old Sol nodded. 'Saw her earlier. Then I seen her knocking on the doc's door a ways back,' he said. 'Not since then, though. Now I think on it I ain't seen the doc, neither.'

It was the first positive piece of news Brad had received. 'Thanks, Sol,' he said and urged his mount on. Outside Doc O'Halloran's surgery he slid quickly from the saddle and hitched the reins to the rail. He ran up the steps and pounded on the door.

The doc came quickly, looking pale. 'Am I glad to see you!' he said.

Brad noticed the worried frown on the doc's face but his own concern caused him to ignore it. 'Where's Kate?'

The doc opened his mouth and closed it several times before he answered. 'I shoulda told the sheriff,' he finally blurted out. 'But my daughter's the only family I have.'

'Told the sheriff what?'

'About Brett bein' shot.'

'That don't worry me none,' Brad said. 'I'm lookn' fer Kate. Have ya seen her?'

Doc O'Halloran took a deep breath and explained all that had happened. 'I shoulda told the sheriff,' he said again, 'but Saul . . . an' then Seth grabbed Kate an' they haven't been back. I'm sorry. I was a coward.'

Brad cut him off. 'Yer sayin' that Seth took Kate away by force an' ya ain't seen them since? Well, I know where that rattlesnake Seth is, an' I'll git the truth outa him.' He strode to the door and wrenched it open. 'I'm obliged.'

He mounted quickly. At the livery he

was told that Seth had already left with two horses. He gazed back up the street and, noticing a small crowd outside the hotel, he rode back towards it, figuring that where there was trouble Saul and Seth could well be the cause.

He arrived in time to see Saul running from the building, leaping on to his horse, and losing no time in putting spurs viciously into its flank. Seth followed and both riders raced away, riding like hell towards him. He watched, as Chas Morgan leaped to safety.

Brad hauled on the reins and held up his hands. 'Stop!' he yelled.

But Saul, his pistol still gripped in his hand, fired. In the poor light and on a running horse it was either a good shot or a lucky one, though unfortunate for Brad. The slug struck him on the left arm, high up, the force and the shock enough to send him tumbling from the saddle into the dirt.

Saul and Seth did not slow down and there were no other folk willing to get in their way. Brad gritted his teeth against the pain, hauled himself to his feet, blood running down his arm. He led his horse across to the hotel entrance where folk were milling about the chaotic scene.

Brad pushed his way through. 'What the hell happened here?' he asked.

Chas Morgan ignored him.

'Where in tarnation is the doc?' someone demanded.

'Ain't nobody goin' after them varmints?' Brad asked.

The deputy looked at him for the first time. 'Oh, it's you. Well, sheriff's bin wounded. A man's bin killed. Mebbe a woman, too. Yeah, we'll git the posse together agin an' we'll catch up with 'em. First, though, we've gotta git the sheriff seen to.'

'I wanna be part of ya posse,' Brad said.

'Seems like ya'll need some attention from the doc yerself.'

At that moment Doc O'Halloran joined them. He was toting his medical

175

bag. 'Where are they?' he asked, his professional demeanour restored.

Chas took him by the arm and urged him into the hotel, but not before the doc had taken note of Brad's injury. He turned back. 'Git yerself down to my surgery. My daughter's there by now. Wait for me.'

* * *

Saul and Seth ran their horses mercilessly. They drew rein eventually under a stand of trees at the top of a bluff. They dismounted and stretched their legs.

'Reckon we bin followed?' Seth asked.

Saul peered back the way they had come. The moon threw an eerie light over the landscape. 'Naw,' he said. 'Too dark to trail us. But they'll be on our heels at first light.'

'We gotta keep moving, then,' Seth said.

'Hosses won't make it 'less we rest

'em fer a while.'

A small rill started its life nearby where water ran from a cleft in the rocks. There was sufficient for the men to fill their Stetsons and allow their mounts to drink. Then they loosened the cinches and let the animals crop the grass.

Seth eyed his companion. 'What was that all about back there?' he asked.

Saul sat and leaned his back against the trunk of a cottonwood. He let his gaze settle on the bag of money hanging from his saddle and wondered how much he could tell Seth.

'Goddamn woman tried to put up a fight,' he said at last. 'Sheriff prob'ly got hisself killed.' He didn't mention that he'd maybe killed the woman, too.

Seth gasped. 'Law's gonna be on our trail fer sure.'

'I guess ya right,' Saul agreed, and was not intending to say more.

Seth was silent for a full minute, but he had clearly been thinking. 'Not a good idea to go chasin' a woman after what happened this morning.'

Saul clenched his fists and pushed himself to his feet, his eyes blazing. 'Trouble with you is ya don't know when to shut yer mouth, nor to keep yer trigger finger still. If you hadn't killed that woman out at the farm we'd've got away with enough cash to keep us goin' fer a while. We got nothin'. You and Brett've allus left it to me to do the plannin' an' that's how it should be. I told ya this morning to keep yer guns in yer holsters.'

Seth didn't back down. 'That ain't fair. I saved yer life.'

'Ya put all our lives in danger.' Saul scanned their back trail again. He could see nothing moving, but he knew he might be deceived by the shifting shadows as clouds flitted across the moon's face. 'I told ya before. Let me do the thinkin' an' you do as I tell ya.'

'What do we do now?' Seth asked.

Saul was beginning to feel that he wanted to get rid of his companion, to go it alone. He was the only one of the three who had ideas. Without him they would have been begging on the streets or robbing old ladies.

'We move on. We got plenty to see us through. We needed cash an' I saw a chance to git some.'

Immediately he regretted what he had said, because Seth's eyes, which had been flicking towards the bag attached to Saul's cantle, now fixed on it. 'How much did ya git?'

Saul hesitated. ' 'Nuff.'

'How much is that?'

'Enough to git us into the next state.'

'An' we share it. Right?'

'Yeah, we share it.' He tried to sound convincing.

Greed glinted in Seth's eyes. 'I should be carryin' half. Safer that way.'

'Safe where it is,' Saul snapped. He had no intention of sharing the money with anyone. Fact was he didn't know how much he had. Substantial, but not enough for two. Nor three, if Brett was counted in, which was not going to happen.

There was a prolonged silence between them. Saul figured to change the subject, get Seth's mind off the idea of money. 'If ya'd been there when I needed ya all this might never have happened an' we wouldn't have to run. Where the hell did ya git to after I left ya at the doc's?'

'Yeah, well, ya should be grateful fer what I did.'

'Oh? An' what was that?' Saul was anxious. He didn't trust Seth. If he had acted on his own initiative there was no telling what damage might have been done.

'Reckoned that might interest you. If I hadn't done it we'd be behind bars now.'

'Goddamn it!' Saul shouted. 'What?'

'Ya sister,' Seth said, obviously intent on stringing this out as far as possible.

Immediately Saul's body went tense. 'Kate? My sister? What about her?'

'She came to the doc's surgery.'

'So?'

'She guessed what we done, how

Brett'd bin shot.'

Saul held his breath, letting it out slowly. 'Go on.'

'Well, I figured she was gonna tell the law.'

'An' just how did ya figure that?'

'She told me.'

Saul felt fear rise in his throat. 'What did ya do?'

'I hit her an' I tied her up. Took her out to that ol' clapboard building on the edge o' town. It ain't used fer nothin' now. Shoulda bin pulled down.'

'Ya tied her up?' Saul's voice was beginning to rise in pitch.

'Yeah, but I hadda put a gag in her mouth. The silly bitch was strugglin' an' shoutin' so loud she coulda bin heard in the next town.'

'Ya left her there?'

'Yeah. Had to.'

'An' ya didn't reckon to tell me?' Saul slowly rose to his feet.

'Tried to, but you was too busy goin' after that dame.'

'Did ya not figure that Kate's my

sister?' Saul's voice now held menace. 'I shoulda known what ya did. Could she've got free by herself?'

Seth still seemed to think he had done the right thing. 'Not a chance. Not the way I tied her. An' I lashed her to a post,' he said proudly.

Saul drew back his fist and drove it into the point of Seth's jaw. 'Ya just left her there!' he screamed as Seth staggered back, tripped and fell. He stepped forward and aimed a vicious kick at Seth's body. 'She's my sister!' he repeated, drawing his foot back for a second strike.

Seth scrambled away. 'She'll be found,' he bleated.

Saul controlled his anger, though his hand was close to his gun butt. 'Mebbe not soon enough. She could be there all night.' Perhaps even he had not fully understood his bond with his sister, but now that her safety was threatened he knew he had to do something about it. He also knew that he wanted to kill Seth, the man who had put her in danger.

He had no doubt that he had the faster draw and he came close to using it, but slowly he relaxed before either man made the move that would ensure that one of them would die.

'She's not gonna be left,' he said.

'Nothin' ya kin do about it now,' Seth growled. 'Anyways, I figured ya not bothered with yer family no more.'

'Ya figured wrong!' Saul strode away and back, trying to get his thoughts in order. Unless she'd been found Kate would already have spent most of the day trussed up without food or water. Now she was about to spend a night unable to move and with the fear that rescue would not save her from a slow death.

He stopped pacing and faced Seth. 'I'm goin' back. If you've harmed her I'll kill ya. No matter where ya've gone, I'll find ya and kill ya.'

'I ain't goin' back,' Seth said. 'Not with the law on our tails. Ya know what'll happen if you're caught.'

'Yeah, but I ain't got no choice. You do what ya want. Go where ya want. My sister can't be left in the hope that someone will find her.' He strode across to his horse, then checked and loaded his Colt. 'Might be needin' this,' he muttered.

Seth grabbed his shoulder. 'How much money ya got there?' He gestured at the bag hanging on Saul's saddle.

'Not your concern,' Saul told him brusquely, and tightened the cinch, ready to mount.

'If you're set on goin' back I'll take my share now.' Seth sounded anxious.

Saul shrugged Seth's hand off. 'An' jus' how much d'ya figure that'll be?'

'A third. I ain't askin' fer more than what's due to me.'

Saul gave a harsh laugh. 'This ain't yours. Nor Brett's.'

'A third. That's fair.'

Saul placed his foot in the stirrup and prepared to mount. 'One dollar's more'n what ya'll get.' As he spoke he sensed rather than saw Seth take a step back and start to draw. He twisted, flung himself down on to one knee and cleared leather in one fluid movement.

Before Seth had brought his .45 level Saul had pulled back the hammer and sent lead into his pard's body. Seth stumbled back, a look of surprise on his face and, with a sigh, he sank down, the gun dropping from his grasp.

'I wasn't gonna . . . ' he began, but was dead before he could finish the sentence.

Saul gazed briefly down at Seth's body. 'Don't matter much now, anyways.'

He lifted the bag down from his horse and stuffed the money into his saddlebags. As a final gesture he took a hundred-dollar note and placed it into Seth's coat pocket.

'Don't say I'm not a generous man,' he grated. He climbed into the saddle and set off at a good pace back towards town. He had considered stashing the saddlebags somewhere for collection later, but on reflection decided they were safer with him. He had no time to bury them and, in the dark, no obvious place to hide them.

The moon appeared only occasionally, causing him to moderate his speed to suit the terrain. As he rode with the cool air driving into his face his thoughts were on Kate. He could do her no good if his horse stumbled and broke a leg.

He and his sister had formed a bond very early on and that bond had not been broken just because he had decided to leave his family. He owed so much to her, for she had been the only one of the family who understood his grief and guilt when his real pa was killed and his ma married again.

His adult life could have been so different. The worst thing was that it had been his fault. If he hadn't kept on calling out to his pa, demanding his attention while he was busting a skittish horse in the corral, his pa would still be alive.

Saul had understood why his ma had

remarried. A woman would find it difficult to run a homestead without the support of a husband and he, Saul, had not been old enough to take on the responsibility of a man.

His new pa had treated him well enough, but his world had shattered at the moment the stallion lashed out.

Now his determination to save his sister overcame all thoughts of his own safety or capture. He urged his horse on.

12

Brad could do little to help with the situation that was developing outside the hotel. He learned from someone that Miles Pitcher had been shot, but whether he was still alive was not known. Another man, newly arrived in town with his wife, had been killed and it was believed that a third person had been shot. Nobody was sure of the details. Different stories swept through the folk watching. If they didn't know for certain they interpreted the events in their own way.

Anyway, Chas Morgan seemed to have it all in hand.

Brad strode down to the doc's house. His arm was now bleeding badly and causing him great pain. He gratefully accepted a neckerchief given to him by someone, which he bound tightly around the wound. When he knocked at the door it was opened by a young woman who could have been no more than twenty. She had a round face that smiled easily. She introduced herself as Gloria, invited him in, adjusted his temporary bandage, and settled him to wait for the doc's return.

He was anxious to get on with the search for Kate, but he had to rest and he had exhausted all the avenues of enquiry that he could think of. Yet there had to be someone who could give an indication of where she had been hidden.

The door to an adjoining room was closed but Gloria went through twice with fresh bandages and it became obvious that a patient was already receiving attention in there.

'Got someone sick?' Brad asked, more as an attempt to start a conversation than through interest.

Gloria stopped what she was doing. 'Pa sees a lot of gunshot wounds these days,' she said. 'Don't know what the town would do without him.'

'Heard there was a shootin' out at one of the farms this morning.'

'I'm not sure whether Brett was involved in that,' Gloria said.

The name made Brad sit up. 'Brett, ya said?'

'I think that's his name. He's resting in the sick room until he's well enough to go out. Now, if you'll excuse me, I must go and tidy up some of Pa's paperwork while I'm here.' Gloria hurried away.

Brad waited for a minute or so, and when Gloria did not return he gave way to temptation and let himself into the sick room. There were four beds, a table, some chairs and a wooden couch which might have been used for treatment. Only one of the beds was occupied.

Brad peered at the occupant and recognized Brett immediately. He was pale but awake and sat up quickly when he saw Brad standing over him. 'What ya doin' in here?' he demanded.

'I want information,' Brad said sharply.

'I got nothin' to say to ya,' Brett snarled. 'Now leave me alone.' He lay back on his pillow and closed his eyes.

Brad leaned closer. Now he was here, with Brett unable to escape, he was going to make use of the situation. 'I'm gonna ask ya a question,' he said quietly. 'An' ya gonna answer.' He waited. Brett kept his eyes shut and said nothing. Brad continued, 'Where is Kate? What have ya done with her?'

Brett's eyes opened wide. 'Don't know nothin' 'bout that.'

Brad reached out and began to put pressure on the bandage that Goria had so expertly placed on Brett's shoulder. 'I asked ya a question,' he said.

Brett squirmed. 'What the hell d'ya reckon ya doing?'

'What went on this mornin', with Saul an' Seth?'

'Dunno. Bin holed up in this cot. I heard voices, that's all. Find Saul or Seth, they'll tell ya.'

'Yeah, I'll ask 'em,' Brad snapped, 'just as soon as I kin find them. Seems like they ran out on ya like the cowardly coyotes they are. Fer now I'm askin' you. If she's come to any harm I'll make sure ya bleed to death.' His finger probed harder.

Brett screamed. 'Goddamn it, ya hurtin' me.'

'I meant to,' Brad said, but withdrew as the door opened and Gloria rushed in, alerted by the screams.

Her expression was concerned. 'What's going on?'

'Nothin',' Brett told her. 'Brad was jus' leaving.'

'You shouldn't be in here at all,' Gloria said.

'Sorry,' Brad said. 'Just thought I heard Brett call out. Must've bin mistaken.' He left the room, sat and waited impatiently outside for the doc to return. When he did he was followed by men carrying makeshift stretchers on which were two bodies, partly covered by sheets.

Brad moved aside as the casualties were taken past him and into two separate rooms. The first he had recognized as Sheriff Miles Pitcher, who was conscious and complaining that he was well enough to walk. The second was plainly a woman, but unrecognizable with her head covered in bloody bandages.

'Be with you shortly,' Doc O'Halloran said as he passed, and Brad sat down again. It occurred to him that Miles Pitcher might be able to come up with some idea to help him in his search for Kate. Chas Morgan had given him nothing. So Brad curbed his impatience as best he could in the hope of questioning the sheriff.

In all his enquiries so far he had reached a dead end. If he went chasing after Seth, who seemed to be the person who had last seen Kate, it could be days before he caught up with him. Too late. Brett maybe knew more than he was saying, and Brad was determined to spend more time with him.

'How's the sheriff?' he asked, as the doc reappeared.

'Not so bad as it looked. Bullet passed right through. He'll be laid up fer a while.'

'Kin I speak to him?'

'Let me tend to that arm o' yours, then I'll ask him. He's an ornery cuss. Wouldn't let me give him anything fer the pain. Says he needs to be alert. Dunno what for.'

Brad removed his vest and shirt to reveal where the slug had torn the flesh. 'What about the woman?'

The doc raised his eyebrows. 'If she'd been an inch taller she'd be dead. Slug creased her scalp. She'll mend.'

He examined Brad's wound while he spoke, then made a few non-committal remarks. He straightened up. 'You're lucky,' he said. 'You mightn't be using that arm fer a while, but no permanent damage. My daughter'll dress it, then ya can go on your way.'

'Thanks, Doc,' Brad said. 'Looks like ya bein' kept busy.'

Doc O'Halloran wiped his brow. 'If it goes on at this rate I'll have to get permanent assistance. Gloria just helps out. Mebbe even have to expand the premises.'

Gloria, young as she was, showed that she was efficient and had done this sort of work before. She cleaned his wound, put some liquid on that hurt like hell, then she bandaged it neatly.

He thanked her and was rewarded with a smile. He looked over at the doc and gestured towards the connecting door. 'What about it, Doc? Will the sheriff see me?'

Before he received an answer they had a visitor, a man wearing a silver star.

'Name's McQuade,' he announced. 'Scott McQuade. Marshal over at Redstone Creek.'

'Long way outa ya bailiwick, ain't ya, Marshal?' the doc asked.

'Yep,' McQuade said. 'Miles Pitcher's expectin' me. I bin told he managed to git hisself in the way of a slug an' you got him here. Like to speak to him.'

'Popular man,' the doc said. 'I'll go see.'

Brad and McQuade sat for a while. 'Reckon I've mebbe had a wasted journey,' the lawman said, as if for the need of breaking the silence.

'Yeah? What's yer business here?'

'The man I was chasin' got hisself killed. He skedaddled with a heap o' money. Some of it mine.'

'Ya rode all the way?'

'Nope. Came by train. Easiest way to travel. Saves a helluva lot o' saddle wear. An' quicker, too.' He laughed. 'Now I need to pay my respects to Miles Pitcher afore I find mysel' a bed fer the night.'

At that moment the medic came back into the room. 'You can go in now,' he told McQuade. 'But keep it quiet. I got other patients to consider. Everything's under control at the moment, an' I'd prefer it to stay that way.' He brushed back errant strands of hair from his forehead. 'Dammit, but it's bin a busy day.'

Brad stood. 'I'm goin' in with McQuade.'

The doc seemed to be about to object, but Brad did not falter and followed the lawman through the door.

Miles Pitcher was sitting up, looking pale but alert. Brett was lying still with his head on the pillow, but Brad formed the impression that the man was feigning sleep. He pulled up a stool and both men sat close to the sheriff. They spoke softly.

McQuade introduced himself. 'This ain't bin a very successful trip,' he said. 'Journeyin' ain't my idea o' fun. I'll be startin' back day after tomorrow. Gotta find out if there's any trace o' the dollars the lawyer was s'posed to be carryin'. Yer deputy says he'll let me know. Kin ya trust him?'

Miles nodded. 'Guess so. He knows better'n to try to pull the wool over my eyes.'

'Ya hurt bad?' McQuade asked.

Miles grimaced. 'Not sufficient to

keep me here fer long. Nobody to blame but myself. Chas Morgan was s'posed to lock up that damned lawyer like I told him to. I was away dealin' with two killin's. When I got back I let the lawyer persuade me to allow him to see his wife. I went with him an' we ran into trouble.'

'You're alive. The lawyer's dead.'

'Yeah, there's somethin' in that. Anyways, I managed a few words with the young lady they just carried in while we were waiting to be brought here. She mumbled something about there being stacks o' high-value dollar bills in her cases that she didn't know nothin' about.'

McQuade sat up. 'Figures. Where's the money now?'

'Dunno. Seems likely Saul might've taken it with him when he rode off.' Miles gave a brief explanation of events. 'You'll be lookin' fer it, then?'

'Yeah,' McQuade agreed.

'Mebbe ya won't be goin' back empty-handed. 'Course, any money'll have to be tallied an' recorded an' accounted fer an' signed fer, all legal. I hope ya get what ya came fer.'

'Yep,' McQuade said. 'That money's owed to a whole heap o' folk. Me included. It'll take some time to git sorted.'

Brad couldn't keep silent any longer. 'Don't care much about yer money. But I do need to talk to Seth.'

The sheriff gritted his teeth. 'Chas Morgan'll git a posse together at sunup. No good tryin' to follow now.'

McQuade showed interest. 'Mind if I tag along? I've gotta big stake in this. Need a good horse, though. The poor-lookin' critter I hired at the station ain't up to it.'

'Yer welcome,' Miles said. 'Those varmints are gonna be caught an' tried in a proper court of law. An' they'll be hung if they're found guilty. Sorry, Brad, I know Saul's family.'

'It ain't that,' Brad said. 'I need to find out where that rattlesnake Seth has hidden Kate. Seems he's the only one who knows. By the time the posse's caught up with him it could be too late.'

Miles Pitcher looked hard at him. 'I cain't help ya there. Wish I could.'

'I'll keep askin' around,' Brad said. He rose from the stool and turned to go. As he did so Brett called to him. He went across and stood looking down with pitiless eyes. 'Whadya want? I ain't got time to spend on you.'

'I heard some of what ya was saying,' Brett said. 'They left me here. I hope ya catch up with 'em.'

Brad waved an impatient arm. 'Don't blame 'em fer leavin' ya. I woulda done the same.'

'They were the ones that did all the killin'.'

'Looks like you'll be the one who'll be hangin' fer 'em.' Brad backed away.

'Wait!' Brett called. 'What I'm sayin' is, I might be able to help ya.'

Brad felt his heart beat faster. 'Yeah?'

'I gotta idea where Seth might've taken yer sister.'

This time Brad leaned over the other

man, stared hard into his eyes. Was this some sort of trick? 'Go on.'

'If I tell ya I need ya to promise to help me. I know the law'll say I did the killin's, but I didn't. You'll have to speak to the sheriff . . . '

He trailed off into a whimper because Brad had grasped his wounded shoulder and had begun to squeeze.

'I ain't gotta do anything,' Brad hissed. 'If you got somethin' to tell me ya'd better start talking.'

'You're hurtin' me,' Brett squealed.

Brad's eyes blazed. 'I ain't even started. Ya ain't felt a thing yet. What ya got to tell me?'

'Ya gotta promise.'

Brad released his grip. 'I'll do what I can, but ya have to understand that the sheriff ain't one who persuades easy.'

Brett took a deep breath. 'There's an old clapboard building, built almost afore the rest of Elsewhere sprang up. On the trail out from the east end o' town. It's fallin' down an' nobody uses it no more. Saul and Seth used to go there sometimes.'

'Did Seth hurt her?'

'Dunno about that.'

Brad straightened up and swung round. It was a small hope, but the only one he had.

'Where ya goin' in such an all-fired hurry?' McQuade asked.

Brad told him, impatient to go.

'I'll go with ya,' McQuade said. 'I ain't doin' nothin' else.'

'You're outa yer jurisdiction here.'

'I ain't got nothing else to do an' mebbe I can help,' the marshal said, and followed Brad out through the door.

13

Kate was scared, thirsty and tired, but scared first and foremost because she knew she was likely to die here in this vermin-infested place. She had no thought of being hungry. She had a good idea where she had been taken, and she had had glimpses of the outside world through gaps in the rotting woodwork on the walls. Now that it was night she could see nothing. Occasionally a horse and rider had gone by, but too far away to take notice of any noise she was able to make.

It had taken her the best part of two hours to work the gag loose and spit out the cloth from her mouth, but it had done her little good except to help her breathe more freely. Her struggles to release her bonds had proved both painful and futile, for Seth had secured her hands and feet with wire and then bound her to a thick pole which had once supported an upper floor.

The blow on the head that Seth had inflicted upon her still gave her pain. She had not fully regained consciousness until Seth had carried her into the building. Then, when she realized what was happening to her, she had put up a valiant fight, but to no avail. Seth was too strong.

'Why are you doing this?' she had asked, as he half-dragged, half-carried her into the building.

'Stop complainin'. Ya'll be safe,' Seth had growled.

'But why?'

'Ya know too much.' Seth tightened his grip on her arm.

'I don't know anything. And you're hurting me.'

'Stop strugglin', then.'

'My head hurts. How long are you keeping me here?'

'Dunno. I'll tell Saul where ya are. He'll know what to do with you.'

'Saul will kill you for doing this.'

Seth had hauled her to the pole and sat her on the hard-baked floor that was covered with some loose dirt and straw blown in by the wind. 'He'll unnerstand why I hadda keep ya quiet fer a while.' He took her arms, forced them behind the pole and bound her wrists together.

Kate was about to argue some more when Seth tore a strip from her shirt and stuffed it in her mouth. Then he took off his neckerchief and tied it tightly round her head. 'Don't want ya callin' out.'

As Seth had cast a last look at her she saw lust in his eyes and, for a brief minute, she feared he might have other ideas. Then the moment had passed and she was alone. She tested her bonds, twisting her wrists and ankles in an attempt to get them free, but Seth had done his job well. All she achieved was to rub the flesh raw. Warm blood trickled down her fingers. Her head dropped from pure exhaustion.

Being confined there in daylight

would have been bad enough. Darkness was worse. The faint rustlings of tiny creatures were magnified and her imagination filled in the rest. But, as the hours went by and she realized that nobody was about to come and save her, she was determined she was not going to give up.

★　★　★

Saul spurred his horse on, taking advantage of the moon whenever it appeared from behind the clouds and cast its intermittent light on the trail ahead. He knew exactly where Seth had put Kate. He knew it could be cold at night, the wind cutting through the cracks and gaps where planks had warped or rotted away. Worse still, he knew the area was infested with vermin and that Kate would probably be unable to keep them off.

As he neared the building, silhouetted against the night sky, he slowed his mount to a walk. Twenty yards away he dismounted, trailed the reins and went forward warily on foot. He waited and listened before pushing open the door and stepping inside.

'Kate,' he called quietly. Then louder, 'Kate, are you there?' He was answered by a groan in the darkness. 'Kate, I'm coming.' He took a vesta from his pocket and struck it with his thumb. The light from the flames was almost lost in the dark but, before it burned his fingers, he saw the shadowy figure slumped on the floor.

'Kate!' The word burst from him. He took a step forward but froze when he heard the sound of the hoofs of two horses approaching from the direction of the town. He stood still, expecting the riders to go on by. Instead they pulled their horses to a stop right outside the door. Two men. He recognized the voice of one of them immediately. 'Brad!' he breathed and stepped back into the gloom.

★　★　★

Brad, with McQuade following, had run outside the doc's and leaped into the saddle. He set off quickly, not bothering whether McQuade was there or not. His heart beat fast as he raced his horse down the short distance to the building that Brett had described.

Clouds covered the night sky as he pulled on the reins and drew to a stop. He slid to the ground. McQuade was only a second behind.

'Take it slow,' the lawman said. 'We dunno who or what's waitin' fer us.'

Brad was not so cautious. 'I'm goin' in,' he said, and led the way.

It was pitch black and he reached into his vest pocket for a match, brought it to life and peered into the gloom. He saw Kate almost immediately and rushed to her, kneeling down beside her, lifting her chin. He placed his hand on her forehead.

'Kate,' he breathed. He felt for a pulse in her neck. 'Thank God you're still alive.'

She did not respond.

The match fluttered out and he reached for a second but, before he struck it, another match flared. He thought it must be McQuade until a voice he knew only too well came out of the shadows.

'How is she?'

Brad barely glanced up. 'Saul! What the hell? I need yer help.' He was feeling for the bonds that held Kate's arms behind the pole. 'Goddamn it! It's wire!' he growled. He heard Saul strike another match. 'Bring that light over here.' He leaped to his feet and kicked at the loose boarding on the wall. It gave way easily and a faint glow from the moon came through the gap.

Saul came across, firing up another vesta. 'How is she?' he repeated.

'Bring that light closer! She's OK. Leastwise, she's breathing. Gotta get her outa here quick an' back to the doc's.'

They both worked frantically at the twisted wire. 'Did you have anythin' to do with this?' Brad asked, anger and frustration mixed in his voice.

'Seth's idea,' Saul said. 'Hell, Kate's my sister. I wouldn't harm a hair of her head.'

McQuade, more cautiously, had entered the building a full half-minute behind Brad.

'Smoke!' he yelled urgently. 'Where in tarnation's that comin' from?'

It soon became plain that Saul, in dropping his first match, had failed to extinguish it, and the dry debris blown against the wall had ignited easily. McQuade raced across and beat at the flames with his coat. The night breeze that had sprung up fanned the fire and he was losing the fight.

'We'll have to hurry,' he said. 'I cain't stop it.'

Brad and Saul redoubled their efforts, forgetting their hatred for each other in their determination to get Kate out alive. Brad felt the ends of the wire bite into his hands, but he was winning. He wouldn't give up now, even as he felt the searing heat on his exposed skin.

The flames spread amazingly swiftly, now shooting up to the rotting roof timbers. Glowing debris fell down on the men. As Brad tried to shield Kate with his body he felt hot embers scorching his head and neck.

'Hurry,' McQuade said again. He raced outside to check on the horses. There was little else he could do to help the other two men.

Neither Brad nor Saul spoke, all their efforts now on the last twists of the wire. As the bonds fell away Brad placed his arms under Kate and lifted her. He felt no weight, only relief, as he ran from the inferno with Saul following behind. Their mounts were showing signs of fear as the heat from the flames spread outwards.

He handed Kate to the lawman while he leaped into the saddle, then took her limp body and held her firmly in front of him. He touched spurs to flesh and set his horse back along the trail.

Behind him the old building had seen

its last days as flames shot up and cast a red glow into the night sky. He hardly noticed it.

As he drew up outside the surgery he was surprised to see that both McQuade and Saul had followed him. He slid from the saddle, kicked at the doc's door and waited impatiently for the medic to appear.

'Bring her in,' the doc said, then, without asking questions, turned and led the way in. 'Now get outa my way while I do what I've bin trained fer.'

Brad turned to go, then heard Brett calling his name. He stepped into the room where Brett was sitting up in bed, grinning.

'I reckon I kept my side o' the bargain, din't I?' he said. 'Ya promised to do what ya kin fer me.'

'Yeah, I said somethin' like that,' Brad agreed.

'Ya gotta keep yer word.'

'I'll talk to the sheriff. Dunno whether he'll listen, though.'

Brett put out a hand and grasped

Brad's arm. 'Saul's out there, ain't he? Tell him I wanna see him.'

Brad shook him off. 'Tell him yerself. I an't yer messenger.'

'He left me here. They both did. I'll git even with 'em. What's he doin' out there?'

Brad was in no mood to respond and, with a brief nod to Miles Pitcher, he reluctantly left the room. He had noticed that Doc O'Halloran was looking drawn and tired and he realized with a shock that he, too, was feeling the strain of a long day. With Kate safely in skilled hands he could relax a little. Before he eventually retired for the night he would wait around to be certain that he had found Kate in time for her to make a complete recovery.

As he entered the outer room his head was down and he did not immediately see McQuade, who was slumped in a sitting position, propped up against a wall cabinet.

'What the hell?' Brad said.

'You might ask,' McQuade said,

rubbing his head.

'I did ask! Where's Saul?'

'Yeah, I'd like to know that. Pistol-whipped me afore I knew what was coming. Ran out as if all the demons in hell were after him.'

'How'd ya let him do that?'

'Must be gettin' slow. I asked him some questions an' he seemed to think I knew more than I did.'

'I'm gonna catch that sonofa — ' Brad grated. He rushed to the door, flung it open and hurried outside in time to see Saul spurring his mount up the main street. As he watched he saw Chas Morgan step in front of the running horse. The deputy was in the process of drawing his gun to add emphasis to his command for Saul to stop when Saul swerved directly at him.

Chas sprang to one side as he realized what Saul's intention was, but a flying hoof caught him on the shin and he spun to the ground, clutching his leg, his Colt slipping from his hand.

'Goddamn it!' Brad muttered, and

sprang into the saddle of his own horse. His injured arm was giving him considerable discomfort and he knew that blood was seeping out from the wound. He tried to ignore it as he urged his horse to more speed. Saul was maybe only 150 yards ahead, but he was going fast and the light from the moon was fitful. 'Mustn't lose him,' he told his mount, and urged it in pursuit.

14

The chase took him along the street out to the main trail, past the glowing remains of Kate's erstwhile prison. Brad considered drawing his Winchester and trying for a shot, but firing from a running horse held no promise of any accuracy. Also, the man ahead was the brother of the girl he loved. Loved? He smiled wryly as, even though he was travelling at high speed, that word had popped into his mind. In any case, he had no wish to kill Saul. He had to stand trial for his misdeeds.

They had travelled for upwards of a mile when Brad noticed that Saul's horse was slowing. His own mount was fresh, eager to go, and could keep going at this pace for a while yet before having to ease down. He guessed that Saul had already ridden some distance and was now trying to push his horse beyond its capability. But he also wondered why he hadn't selected a fresh animal from those hitched outside the doc's.

'Sure,' he muttered to himself. 'Ya still got the money, ain't ya?' He intended to find out for certain when he caught up. For now the important thing was to stay close enough to keep him in view.

Brad eased his pace, saving the horse's stamina for the final rush, but maintaining the distance between the two men, waiting for Saul to realize that escape was not going to be possible. He withdrew his Colt and fired a warning shot into the air.

Saul responded by turning in his saddle and loosing off a shot that went wide. Brad fired again, knowing that if he wanted to he could bring his brother down. But his intention was not to kill. He had to play a waiting game, while at the same time preventing Saul from getting off a lucky shot.

He fired for a third time. It had no

effect. Perhaps after all it was time to bring this chase to a conclusion.

He realized that delaying the inevitable had been a mistake when he saw that Saul, knowing that he could not outrun his pursuer, was angling off over rough ground towards a stand of cottonwoods. Perhaps it was there that Saul intended to make a stand.

Brad followed but, as Saul neared the trees, he slowed and approached cautiously. He drew in a sharp breath as Saul suddenly disappeared.

Brad drew rein. 'What in tarnation?' he mumbled.

It soon became clear that Saul had dropped into an arroyo, which was concealed by thick vegetation. Had he meant to do this? Did he know the layout of the land hereabouts and was leading Brad into an ambush? Whatever the answers might be Brad knew he had to be careful.

He set his horse at an angle that he hoped would intercept Saul if his intention was to race along the riverbed, or would enable Brad to circle around his brother's position. He listened but heard nothing. He reached the bank without incident, slid to the ground and edged forward with gun drawn. When he reached a position where he could peer down into the gully he saw Saul's horse, clearly favouring one leg and, beyond that, Saul lying on the stony ground where he had been thrown.

Brad looked for a way to climb down without losing sight of his quarry. Saul was full of guile, he reminded himself; maybe he was pretending injury, waiting for Brad to lose concentration.

Saul remained still for the time it took Brad to reach him, then he leaped to his feet, his hand already snaking to his holster. Brad, for all his vigilance, was too slow to react. But Saul's hand came away empty, for the six-gun had slipped from his belt and now lay a few feet away from where he stood.

He lunged towards it.

'Don't!' Brad shouted, his own Colt

held firmly and pointing at his brother's chest.

Saul growled. 'Damn you to hell! Think you're smart? I woulda had ya if the damned horse hadn't thrown me.'

Brad merely smiled, relieved that the chase had ended so easily. 'It takes a good man to know when he's beaten,' he said. 'You rode yer horse too hard an' you've come to the end o' the trail. Ya've killed an' robbed an' broken yer parents' hearts. Now I'm takin' ya back to stand trial, though it pains me to do so. Now take a step back.' He went forward and stooped to pick up Saul's gun.

But Saul had only made a show of stepping away. Instead, he sprang forward, his boot coming up and taking Brad under the ribs. The speed and severity of the attack took him by surprise. The power of the blow sent him back, gasping for breath as pain seared his chest.

Saul followed up his attack swiftly with another sweep of his boot that connected with Brad's knee and threw him to the ground. 'You're gonna be pickin' yer teeth outa the dirt,' Saul hissed, as he surged forward again with the intention of inflicting more damage.

Brad had managed to hold on to his gun and, through misty eyes, he fired into the air. 'Step back,' he roared, and gritted his teeth against the agony in his ribs. 'I swear the next slug'll kill ya.'

He scrambled to his feet, wincing at the pain racking his body. 'Fact is I didn't wanna kill ya but I've changed my mind. It's best if yer ma and pa never see ya agin.'

Even as he levelled the gun at Saul's chest he doubted that he could pull the trigger. Perhaps if he gave Saul a chance, man to man, he might be able to do it, even if he put his own life at risk. He took the two weapons and emptied them both of all but one bullet. Saul's gun he laid on the ground, then he paced back several yards.

'Pick it up,' he grated. 'But easy. Very easy. Then place it in yer holster.'

With a puzzled look Saul did as he was told and a grin spread across his face as Brad did the same.

'I'm not a murderer like you,' Brad said. 'I'm givin' ya a chance.'

Saul laughed. 'I only do my killin' when I got a mind to. Now it'll give me satisfaction to kill you. Ya tried to take my place with Ma jus' like my new pa did. Now that's gonna finish.'

Brad shook his head sadly. 'I was never yer enemy. You resented me from the start an' I only wanted to be friends.'

He couldn't be certain how this would finish. He had set off after Saul with no clear ending in mind. Certainly not to kill him. But the alternative of taking him to trial would bring untold suffering to his ma and pa. No doubt they would mourn his own death if it came to that, but better to end it all swiftly.

But the enmity between himself and Saul was going to be settled in a fair fight, although fairness was something that Saul had not exercised for many years.

'Draw when ya ready. I know ya kin shoot defenceless women,' Brad said grimly. 'Let's see what you're like against a man.' He felt no fear or elation that this moment had arrived, no joy, but the desire to see justice done.

Saul made no move.

'I'm not goin' agin ya,' he muttered. 'I know you're fast with that gun an' I've no mind to die here.' Very slowly, with the finger and thumb of his left hand, he withdrew the gun and let it fall. 'Ya wouldn't shoot an unarmed man, would ya?'

'You've made it easy fer me, ya lily-livered skunk,' Brad said. 'I gave you a chance. Now give me a reason not to kill ya.' His eyes were misted with anger and frustration.

'Ya haven't the guts to pull the trigger against an injured man, that's why,' Saul said. He bent over as if in pain and rubbed his leg. 'I'm hurt,' he groaned. 'I

223

hurt myself when my goddamned horse threw me, so it wouldn't be a fair fight. I need the doc.'

Brad watched him carefully, expecting him to pick up his gun again, but he straightened up without doing so, and Brad relaxed. Saul's injuries were probably real.

'We're goin' back to town,' he said. 'You'll be walkin' in front if ya horse ain't fit to ride.'

'I ain't goin' back,' Saul whined. 'I can't go back. They'd hang me sure as hell. I'd rather die here.'

Brad had the very briefest glimpse of moonlight on metal as the thin-bladed throwing knife left Saul's hand and flashed towards him. His instinctive reaction saved his life as he leaned to one side, but the blade struck him in the flesh of his shoulder, close to his existing wound, and it stayed there.

Saul, with a grunt of triumph, scooped up his gun and thumbed back the hammer. In the act of his pulling the trigger the bullet from Brad's Colt struck him in the side and his own shot sped harmlessly into the air. Saul sank to his knees while Brad struggled to reload his weapon.

With a great effort he pulled the knife from his arm. He took off his bandanna and thrust it under his shirt, where fresh blood was already staining the material.

'Damn you to hell!' he gasped. 'On yer feet. I'd rather shoot ya when you're standing, but if ya give me any more tricks any way'll suit me.' His eyes were without pity.

Saul snarled and, holding his side, struggled to his feet. He stood facing Brad defiantly, knowing he had used up all the chances he was going to get.

Brad cocked the gun. His finger rested on the trigger but remained without moving. The final twitch that would have sent Saul into eternity never came. He thought of Sam and Sadie, who had taken him in and treated him well. He thought of Kate, Saul's sister. What would she have wanted him to do? And last of all he thought of himself and how he could never shoot a man, however bad, in cold blood.

Taking great care in case Saul had more tricks up his sleeve, he bound Saul's hands behind his back with his own bandanna.

'Lie down!' he said. 'Face on the ground. An' don't move.' When Saul had reluctantly obeyed, Brad examined his horse. He lifted the right foreleg and immediately saw the problem, a sharp flint embedded in its hoof. While he kept Saul in sight he extracted the stone using the point of Saul's knife. He walked the animal around and was satisfied with the result.

'Well, yer lucky,' he said to Saul. 'Ya can ride home. I cottoned on to what made ya so doggone keen to ride off with ya own horse when there were other fresh mounts ya could have had,' he said. 'Don't reckon ya were scared o' gettin' hung for horse-thieving. Mebbe ya got somethin' valuable in ya saddlebags.'

From Saul's reaction he knew he had hit on the truth. He opened each saddlebag in turn, thrust his hand inside and withdrew some of the bundles. He gazed at them in wonder. For a moment he was speechless. A fortune lay there.

'We kin share,' Saul called out. 'There's enough fer both of us. Let me go an' you'll never see me agin. We'll both be rich.'

'I'm guessin' it ain't your money to give away,' Brad said. 'Where'd ya get it?'

Saul wrongly sensed salvation, and hope briefly gleamed in his eyes. 'I found it in that dame's travel bags,' he said, speaking quickly. 'She got offa the coach with her husband. He was taken away by the deputy an' I reckoned to pay her a visit in her room. They musta stolen it.'

'So you stole it from them?'

A grin of satisfaction suffused Saul's face. 'Yep. Reckon I killed him. Mebbe killed the dame, too. She gave me these scratches, the stupid bitch.' He indicated the bloody scores down his cheeks. 'So now the money kin be ours. Yours an' mine.'

'Cain't pretend the offer's not tempting,' Brad said with a smile. 'But, when ya think about it, the money belongs to someone an' I'm damned sure they'll be missing it. Now, you spineless jackass, mount up. I've a notion to make you ride backwards. If ya give me an excuse to shoot you I'll be happy to oblige.'

He transferred the saddlebags to his own horse, then helped Saul into the saddle. 'An' don't get any ideas of fallin' off an' tryin' to get away. If ya do that then you will be walkin'.' He received a disgruntled nod from the other man, climbed stiffly into the saddle and led the way back. As he nursed the pains from the punishment his body had taken he watched Saul's discomfiture with some satisfaction.

15

The ride back gave rise to no further problems and within an hour and a half they reined in outside the law office. A light shone from the window but the door was locked and nobody appeared to be inside. Then Brad remembered that Miles Pitcher was recovering at Doc O'Halloran's surgery and that the deputy, Chas Morgan, had been hurt trying to prevent Saul's escape.

'Looks like nobody's home,' he said. He glanced up at Saul, who was slumped forward and did not appear to have survived the journey well. 'Mebbe get ya treated afore ya see the inside of ya cell.'

He remounted and they rode back up the main street. 'Git down,' he ordered when they were outside the doc's. 'Let's find out if ya still got my slug inside you.'

He pushed open the door and urged Saul inside. The doc, looking more exhausted than ever, was just emerging from the surgery. He took note of Saul's condition with bleary eyes and groaned theatrically. 'How many more are ya gonna bring in?'

'I hope this might be the last,' Brad said. 'Soon as ya've treated him I'll git him safely behind bars. How's the rest of yer patients?'

The doc tried for a smile. 'Ready to get on their way,' he said proudly. 'All except Miles.'

'Kate?'

'She's fine. Fact is she wants to see you. You can talk to her now if you want. She's in the back room. Gloria's made her some chicken broth. McQuade's there, too. If you want some yourself you'd best hurry.'

'I've gotta keep an eye on Saul,' Brad said.

'Sheriff can do that from his bed. He's bin shouting for his pants an' gun fer long enough. I don't cotton to guns in my house but Sam's a mighty determined man.'

Brad helped the doc get Saul on to the couch in the sick room. 'You all right with this, Sheriff?'

Miles Pitcher swung his legs over the side of his bed. 'Time I earned my pay.' He held his Colt on his lap. 'I've dealt with more dangerous critters than him.'

Brad noticed that Brett's bed was empty. 'Where's the waster?'

'He's already left. Glad to be rid of him. He insisted on going. Seemed to have something on his mind. By sunup I'll only have Miles left, an' I'll be able to get about seeing to my other patients out there.'

'You'll have some spare beds, then,' Brad said with a grin.

A tired smile spread across the doc's pale face. 'Promise me you'll not bring in any more casualties. I've already lost a night's sleep.'

'Both young ladies'll be leavin' ya, then?' Brad asked, serious now.

'Yeah. They were no trouble at all.

Fact is I'll be sorry to see them go. They both aim to spend what's left of the night here and leave soon's it's light.'

'Thanks fer lookin' after Kate, Doc. I'm obliged.'

'Thought ya might be,' the older man said with a twinkle in his eye. 'We need to let her ma and pa know she's all right.'

'I'll do that,' Brad said. 'But first I gotta see her.' He followed the doc's directions and walked through to the room at the rear of the building that the medic used for cooking, eating, reading and relaxing. It was small and cosy, an open fire burning in the grate, books lining one wall and comfortable furniture crammed into the rest of the space.

McQuade had seen him come in, but Kate was seated with her back to the door, spooning soup into her mouth, and had not heard his approach. He took the opportunity to stand and gaze at her. The sight of her now, and the feel of her young body as he had carried her earlier, awoke desires that he had subdued for so long.

She sensed his presence and turned round, smiling broadly when she saw who it was.

She laid her spoon in the bowl, stood and rushed towards him. 'Thank you,' she said, and threw her arms around his neck. Her lips found his.

He responded gently. When they parted he said, 'Well, if that's the reward I get I'll rescue you every day.'

Kate drew back and grinned. 'You don't have to wait to rescue me.'

McQuade rose and made a silent exit. Brad called him back. 'If ya were lookin' fer money, there's a heap o' it in two saddlebags on my horse. Could ya bring 'em in an' mebbe give 'em to the marshal fer safe-keeping?'

McQuade nodded and hurried away.

Brad and Kate sat and talked while Kate finished her soup. 'Why didn't you stay after you brought me in?'

Brad hesitated before replying, not wanting to spoil this moment. 'Sorry, Kate, but I had to go after Saul.'

Kate paled. 'He was there, wasn't he? At the fire.'

'Yeah, Kate. He came back to rescue you after running off with Seth.'

'It was Seth who tied me up.' She fell silent. 'Did Saul have anything to do with that?'

'Kate, I know how close you and Saul have been. I don't reckon he knew what Seth had done 'til later. As I see it he rode back and risked everything when Seth told him. P'raps there's some good in him after all. He's being treated by the doc now. After that he'll go to jail.'

'And after that?'

Brad could not think how to soften his reply. 'He'll face trial.'

Kate spooned in the last of the soup. 'For what?'

'I'm not the law, Kate. He shot an' killed a man, the husband of the woman in there.' He gestured with his thumb. 'Mebbe he kin plead self-defence. I dunno. He had money with him when he was brought in. Saddle-bags stuffed full of it.'

Kate looked away, afraid to meet his eyes. 'He's my brother. Can you help him? Will you help him?' She turned and gazed at him with big, round eyes, pleading.

This meeting was not going the way Brad had hoped. 'I'll do what I can, but the law will have to take its course. Saul has to answer for what he's done.' Even to himself he sounded callous, uncaring. It was not what he was feeling.

Kate's eyes bored into his. 'He's my brother,' she repeated.

'I know, Kate. In a way he's my brother, too. Yes, I'll do everything I can. Not for him. For you. And fer Ma and Pa.'

'If he's hung it'll break their hearts. You could help him escape, couldn't you?'

Brad had promised to do everything possible for this girl, but could he give aid to a killer? He tried to put his own feelings aside. If Saul went free the chances were that more men would die by his gun; if he went before a judge he would inevitably face the rope.

Brad saw no middle course. He wrapped his arms around Kate and held her, feeling her young body tremble. 'I'll do whatever I can, Kate.' Suddenly he was tired, needing to bring the night's events to a conclusion.

'Promise?'

'I promise.' He felt great tenderness, great love, for her. When her lips met his he knew at once that she felt the same towards him. He made up his mind to do whatever was necessary to keep his promise.

He glanced out of the window and was surprised to see a lightening of the sky. The night had almost slipped by unnoticed. Sunup was only a short time away. 'Soon as it's light,' he told her, 'we'll go home and give the news to Ma and Pa.'

Kate was about to reply when they heard voices: the harsh tones of McQuade and a more belligerent reply from Saul.

'Stay here,' Brad said. 'I'll go an' find

out what that's all about.' As he strode out through the door he sensed that Kate was following.

In the front room they saw that McQuade was holding Saul at gunpoint. 'Git movin'. Sooner yer behind bars the quicker I kin get some shuteye.'

'I'm not fit,' Saul snivelled. 'In case ya haven't noticed, I bin shot.'

McQuade shot a glance at the doc and received a nod in answer to his unspoken question. 'Yeah, ya've bin shot. Doc says ya fit to move. An' I'll willingly put another slug in ya if you try anything.'

Kate gasped and ran up to her brother, throwing her arms around him. 'We'll help you,' she told him. 'Whatever you've done we'll help you.'

Saul sneered. 'Don't worry. They won't hold me fer long.'

'That won't be my problem,' McQuade said. 'All I gotta do is lock the cell door.'

Brad stepped forward. 'I'll take him down,' he said.

McQuade continued to urge his

captive towards the door. 'You ain't the law. I am.' He thumbed his silver star.

'Not here, ya not,' Brad argued. 'Yer badge don't mean nothin' in Elsewhere.'

The marshal glared at him and gave Saul a shove that sent him stumbling outside into the night. McQuade followed quickly, his Colt held ready.

Brad caught the door and went out after them. The moon had dimmed and only a few stars remained. The light wind was dying and a new day was not far away. But what would it bring for him if he carried his plan through?

He followed as McQuade and Saul walked the short distance to the jail. When Saul stumbled the lawman jabbed him in the back with his Colt. At the law office McQuade took a key from his pocket and inserted it into the door.

Brad slipped his gun from its holster and stepped in front of the lawman. His pulse was racing. He knew what he was doing was wrong. He was about to let a killer loose, but what choice did he have?

'I cain't let ya — ' he began.

They all froze as a voice, harsh with anger, came out of the dark alley. 'Hold it right where ya are.'

'That's Brett,' Brad said.

Saul jerked himself upright. 'Shoot 'em, Brett! And let's git outa here.'

The roar of a shot, fired at close range, rent the air.

Saul grunted, took two faltering paces back, and collapsed on to the ground.

Brad had seen the flash of the killer's gun coming from the alley and, with his own weapon in his hand, he fired instinctively. A yell of pain and the sound of a body falling could be clearly heard. A man lay unmoving in the half-light.

McQuade leaped forward, his gun drawn, but there was no need for further action. He carefully kicked the gun away before cautiously examining the body. 'He won't be causin' no more trouble,' he announced. 'That was a good shot.'

Brad was already lifting Saul up from the boardwalk. 'More luck than skill,' he admitted. 'Saul's still breathing. We'll have to be quick.'

They started back the way they had come, leaving Brett where he lay.

At the doc's Kate appeared at the doorway as Brad carried Saul in. 'What was the shooting?' she asked. Then she caught sight of Saul's limp body. 'Oh!'

Doc O'Halloran came forward. 'Is there to be no end to this?' he asked.

Brad lowered Saul on to a chair. Kate knelt in front of him.

The doc made a quick examination of Saul's wound, straightened up and shook his head. 'I'll do what I can,' he muttered, while Gloria, appearing as bleary-eyed as her pa, waited for instructions.

Brad looked down at Kate. 'We didn't cotton on to how angry Brett was feeling,' he said lamely. 'I mean, about him being abandoned by his partners.' Whether Kate heard or not he didn't know. And if she did, would she understand? He'd done his best, but it hadn't been good enough.

Saul opened his eyes. They focused on his sister. 'I'm sorry, sis,' he breathed.

'So am I,' Kate said, and held him as he died.

The impatient and angry voice of Miles Pitcher reached them from the other room. 'What in tarnation's goin' on out there? Is nobody gonna tell me?'

This brought a brief smile to the doc's lips. 'Reckon I'll be relieved to see him outa my way.'

With a squeeze of Kate's shoulder Brad said, 'I'll go tell him the news, how we've all managed so well without him. That should cheer him up.'

As he approached the recovery room a young lady emerged from a door further down the corridor. The bandages had now been removed from her head, and her hair, long and flowing, covered the damage she had sustained to her scalp.

Brad nodded a greeting towards her and continued on his way. The sheriff was still yelling at the top of his voice and the doc was saying something.

Brad heard none of it.

He halted in mid-stride, his breathing suspended, his heart beating fast. The world had stopped. Slowly, deliberately, his mind not accepting what he had seen, he swung round.

The eyes of brother and sister met, staring long and hard, unbelievingly, at each other.